With Age Comes…

A Collection of Short Stories
Celebrating Older People

Written by Margot Ogilvie

immortalise

ISBN 978-0-6455379-1-8

Cataloguing-in-Publication entry is available from the National Library of Australia http:/catalogue.nla.gov.au/.

This edition first published in 2022

Typesetting by Ben Morton
Cover art work by Lorraine Lewitska
Cover design by Jonathan Ogilvie

Published in Australia by Immortalise via Ingram Spark
www.immortalise.com.au

Dedicated to:

This book is dedicated to
the very best 'old' person I know – my dad.
I love laughing with you.
I love hearing your stories of days gone by.
I love that you are always there for me, even when we're apart.
I love that your voice is always in my head telling me,
'You've done a great job.'
I love you, Dad.

With many thanks to:

*My family, for putting up with late dinners,
dirty dishes and sloppy housework.
My pre-readers, Lianne, Meredith and Michelle – thanks for loving
my stories and helping perfect them with your detailed feedback.
Lorraine – thanks for giving my characters
such adorable, lovable faces.
Jonathan – thanks for designing an eye-catching cover.
Robert and Elaine Bailey, my personal cheer squad – this book
wouldn't have happened without your encouragement.*

Table of Contents

Introduction

Depending on your age, your health, your financial situation, and so many other factors, you might finish our title with any or all of the following:

Arthritis

Trouble remembering	Love
Loss of independence	Laughter
Incontinence	Wisdom
Trouble seeing	Grandchildren
Loss of drivers licence	Legacy
Trouble hearing	Bucket Lists
Loss of friends	Deep thinking
Swollen legs	New friendships
Trouble moving	Influence
Loss of life partner	Stubborn pride
Thin skin	Time
Trouble balancing	Plenty of good yarns
Loss of appetite	
A plethora of pills	
Trouble healing	
Loss of energy	
Isolation and Loneliness	
Trouble sleeping	

It's that second column we're going to focus on in this book, because hiding inside every 'grumpy old man', every wrinkled elderly lady, there's someone wonderful just aching for you to spend some time with them. Once you do, you'll discover a fountain of wisdom, someone who has learned how to do life by living for a lot of years, through the best and worst of times, and surviving to tell a story that's well worth listening to.

With age comes... plenty of good yarns

In my short time working in aged care, I've been privileged to hear many a good yarn. That's one thing common to most older people – they tend to be generous with their stories, always happy to share them with anybody who takes the time to listen.

I've heard tragic stories, funny stories, sad stories and unbelievable-but-true stories. Stories of courage, love, pain, adventure, perseverance, triumph and joy.

And the amazing thing is that, whilst some stories are tainted with the odd bit of exaggeration, or confounded by the lapsing memory of the teller, each one is based on fact.
The storyteller was really there, living the story, finding the courage, feeling the pain, celebrating the triumph, sharing the love and experiencing the joy.

And sharing that special part of themselves with anybody who'll take the time to listen.
I'm so glad I did.

Filling in Forms

Kathleen

How stupid can people be? Unhelpful! Insensitive! Condescending! Dumb! Thoughtless! Contrary! Impractical! Inconsiderate! Rude!

These are just some of the thoughts raging through my head as I wait for the taxi to take me home at last. My specialist wants me to have a 'minor procedure' (as if there is such a thing at my age!), so I was sent from one department to another to organise things. I never realised just how huge this hospital was until my aching, swollen feet started yelling at me about their need for rest. There were plenty of closed doors, numerous blank faces at counters, and more than enough queues everywhere I turned, but nowhere near enough seats. Sure I could've sat on my walker when my legs refused to take another step, but it wouldn't have been long before other, more bulky parts of my body started complaining.

The short version of the story is that there are forms to be filled in. And lots of them. One ridiculously skinny young lass, with a purple stripe in her hair, if you don't mind, offered to email me a link to the online version, so I could fill it in, print it, sign it and scan it to email back to her. I told her she'd left out a few vital steps that would stop me getting the forms back to her in a timely manner. She'd need to help me buy a computer, and a printer, then

1

teach me how to use them and so on. She stared at me as if I was from another planet, picking up her dropped jaw in time to say, 'You mean you don't have a computer.'

'No, dear, I don't.'

'Well, you could always do it on your phone.'

I shook my head, my patience wearing thin. This little twit just didn't get it. I tried to explain with, 'Except that my phone has one end for talking and one for listening, and just enough buttons to dial a number. No screen, nowhere to plug in a printer.'

'Oh,' she still looked blank. 'What sort of mobile is that?'

I was sorely tempted to walk away as fast as my throbbing feet would take me, but that wouldn't get the surgery happening. 'Do the forms come on paper, by any chance?' I made a huge effort and smiled nicely.

'I suppose I could print them off for you.'

'Why, thank you. That's a wonderful idea.' The poor girl was so daft she didn't catch on to my sarcasm, although she certainly knew how to use her computer and, quick as a flash, thrust a huge wad of forms in my direction, along with a reply paid envelope.

Not even taking the time to look at them, I shoved them in my already-too-heavy handbag and made my way slowly to the exit to hail a taxi.

The longer I wait, the more disappointed I am with my attitude. I'm not usually such a negative person. Over our nearly seventy years together, Bob often referred to me as a 'glass-half-full' person, especially when my joyfulness got on his nerves. But I'm tired. My feet hurt all the way to my waist. And I'm facing the prospect of all those forms, and the surgery to follow, alone.

Home and a nice cup of tea beckon. Bob won't be there, but I've got to get used to managing on my own.

Skye
What a day! I left home just after eight, helped three people with showers, prompted two lots of medication, made a total of five beds with clean linen (none of them my own), took someone shopping and cleaned two houses (again, not my own) – all in a Covid-safe mask, in 85% humidity and thirty-three-degree heat. And I'm not finished yet.

I pull into Kathleen's drive, my last client of the day. I wonder if she's back from her appointment in the city yet. Before leaving the car, I reach for the body spray I keep in the glove compartment and apply it liberally – I need all the help I can get today. I give my hair a quick primp and take a big breath, releasing it slowly before donning the dreaded mask, straightening my shoulders and pasting a smile on my face, obviously more for my benefit than hers.

My motto as a home support worker has always been, 'every client deserves to feel special, and receive my best care.' Today, as I repeat it all the way to the door, I add, 'even after a very long, very hard, very muggy day.'

Kathleen
I make the tea, but can't relax and enjoy it until the blessed forms are done. Pushing the fine china tea cup that was a wedding present sixty-eight years ago out of the way, I dig the wad of papers out of my discarded handbag. Why do they insist on making the print on these things so tiny?

The five minutes I spend searching for my glasses, followed by the next five spent cleaning them is time sadly wasted, because I

3

still can't read the questions. Despite loud protests from my throbbing knees, I get up and turn the light on, even though it doesn't seem dark in the room yet. That doesn't help either.

Picking up my now lukewarm tea and the sheaf of papers, I amble out to what is usually my afternoon sanctuary – a place bathed in afternoon sunshine, where therapeutic warmth soaks right through joints aching with age; where I so often find comfort and solace in a large print book from the mobile library; where I am regularly lulled into a late afternoon snooze, filling that slow part of the day before the evening news with dreams of better days long past – my sunroom.

Bob had never quite finished closing in our back porch, but, oh, how he'd loved tinkering away at each little part of the project. Perhaps that's why I love it here so much.

But today, it's no sleepy haven of healing warmth and pleasant memories. Today, there's work to be done, and the bright sunlight I find waiting for me allows me to read the questions with only minimal eye strain. If only I'd brought a pen. I hobble back into the kitchen and test four pens, freebies from long-closed businesses, before I find one that works.

Back out in the sunroom, I discover another flaw in the forms. Although the first question is basic – my name – my effort to fit the letters into the outrageously small squares exacerbates the tremor in my hand, leaving me ashamed that my best effort is barely readable. And I know what it says! My name looks like it's been scratched out by a bird writing in the sand. I've missed some squares completely.

More than a few people during my life have referred to me as stubborn. I like to think of it more as persistence, something which has served me well over the years. It's the only thing that keeps me going past the address section. Next comes my Medicare Number. That requires another trip back into the house.

My whingeing feet divert me to the bedroom for my slippers, which really need a wash to freshen them up. I stand in the passage for a while, basking in the comfortable silence emanating from my finally-satisfied feet, and temporarily puzzled over why I left the sunroom. Finally, it comes to me and I retrieve my purse and return to the dazzling warmth I love.

My purse is bulging with cards of all colours and types. There are bank cards, government cards, rewards cards for businesses I don't even remember going to once, let alone frequenting enough times to warrant the number of holes punched in them. If at least three of the cafes were still in business, they'd owe me three free coffees. I wonder?

I pull out five green coloured cards, three of which say Medicare. I scrawl the number into the squares provided and the expiry date of the first one I come to. After squeezing more details into more tiny squares, I celebrate completing an entire page with a sip of long-cold tea, wishing Bob were here to share the moment. Then, with a shake of my trembling, aching hands, I turn the page.

Skye
There's no answer at Kathleen's front door, which is nothing new. It happens fairly often, when she forgets to put her hearing aids in, when she's nodding in front of the afternoon game shows, or when she's busy with a project. Perhaps I can make myself heard from the back door, if she's even home. I've only been allocated fifteen minutes to administer her evening medications and make her some

dinner, so I walk as quickly as possible along the cluttered side path, dodging wheelie-bins, rose bushes and garden hoses.

I gasp at the sight awaiting me in the little closed-in back porch. In place of the feisty, independent, I-can-manage-without-help-thanks-all-the-same woman I usually encounter at this address is an exasperated, despondent figure slumped over a rickety card table, which has been sloshed by the spilled contents of a haphazardly placed cup and saucer. Surrounded on both floor and table by what appears to be the scattered contents of her ancient purse, she's scratching away at a form of some sort, muttering something about 'more stupid questions'.

'Blinking forms,' she hisses, loud and clear this time, although I'm not certain whether she even knows I'm here.

'Hello, Kathleen. What seems to be the trouble?'

Rather than a greeting of any sort she simply says, 'You any good at filling in forms?'

I can't seem to lie to save myself so I say. 'Yes, I love form-filling.'

She hands me the pen.

Because, of course, Kathleen being Kathleen, it has to be done NOW.

I settle into the rickety bamboo chair and soon find myself sorting through half a dozen DVA cards looking for one that's current. My time is fast running out, but Kathleen will fret, and lose sleep if we don't get these forms more-or-less done tonight. So, I repeat question after question, over and over again, wishing for multiple reasons that I could take off the mask.

Half an hour later, perspiration running down my back, knowing I'm well-and-truly pushing the limits anyone can hope for from a few squirts of body spray, I wonder again why we are out here on the not-even-finished, fully-sunned, fully-glassed back porch. I'm fairly certain I've pushed dear Kathleen as far as I can for answers. She's had a huge day, and she's fed up with the whole thing. Although her mind is pretty good, she is ninety-eight, and she's seemed a little fuzzy on the last few answers.

Relieved, I realise I'll have to refer to the Home Care Folder for the rest of the form – finally an excuse to get out of this sauna.

Kathleen
At first, I resented the stream of ladies coming through my house, but right now, I'm more grateful to see Skye than I have ever been to see anyone. Especially when she said she'd help with the blessed forms. And she's breezed through it, reading out the questions, and filling in my answers.

Now we've gotten to some harder ones, and she wants to go inside. I'm loving the warmth and brightness of the sunroom, and she wants me to go into the cool gloom of the house. Still, if it gets the forms done, I'll be able to sleep tonight, and relax. The time off my feet hasn't stopped the pain heading straight back there as soon as I stand up.

I can't wait to go to bed.

Skye
The forms are done, except for a few details the office will need to supply tomorrow. I won't tell Kathleen, or she'll still worry. Can't have mere formalities like power of attorney and medication lists robbing a sweet elderly lady of precious sleep.

I'm way over time, but she still needs her evening pills and something for dinner. Even allowing for her tiredness, she doesn't seem her usual spirited self, and I don't feel it's right to rush away just yet. She puts on a good show most of the time, but I know she misses her husband, Bob. Probably even more than usual with surgery hanging over her head.

'What do you fancy having for tea, Kathleen?'

'A cuppa sounds good to me, dear. And perhaps I'll make a piece of toast later.'

'How about I make the toast for you now, and maybe even poach an egg to go with it?'

'Ooh, would you, dear? I haven't had a poached egg in ages. You know, that used to be Bob's specialty on a Sunday morning. The only time he ever cooked. Except for barbeques, of course.'

While she proceeds to detail Bob's egg-poaching secrets, I boil the kettle to get things happening as fast as possible, hoping my hard-working husband might be persuaded to settle for cooking himself a poached egg, or maybe two, because I'm way too tired to cook anything more respectable.

Finally, I settle Kathleen at the table, with a nice hot cup of tea, and what I know will only ever be considered an average poached egg. We both know it won't be as good as Bob would have made, but I truly hope seasoning it with a journey down poached-egg-and-barbeque-memory-lane has enhanced the experience. Rather that than have the memories-turn-to-missing sour the taste of my efforts in her mouth.

I fill in the progress notes, and collect my keys and phone.

'Time I got going, Kathleen. Will you be okay now? Nessa will be here in the morning to help you through the morning routine.'

'Yes, dear, I won't be long out of bed tonight. I'm done in.'

'Well, that's completely understandable after such a huge day. You sleep well, and I'll see you next time. Don't worry about those forms. Jill from the office will be able to fill in those few missing details really easily tomorrow when she visits at 11 o'clock.'

'Okay, Thanks so much, dear. You're a Godsend. You came along just when I needed you.'

I resist the urge to place a kiss on her forehead. The cantankerous client who greeted me earlier is gone, and even the lively lady I'm used to has been mellowed by fatigue and concern. All that remains is a tired, lonely soul, softened by appreciation for a need met.

I get into my car, still bone-tired, but supremely satisfied that I was there to meet her need; that I'd made a positive difference to Kathleen's evening; that I'd done my job and done it well.

Kathleen

I really can't be bothered with the evening news tonight. As soon as I finish my cuppa, I struggle into my nightie and sink into bed. It's so nice to finally and fully have the weight off my feet. As usual, I revisit the events of the day, just as Bob and I used to as we lay spooning together on our way to sleep.

I'd been worried about those forms, but Skye had made it seem so easy. There's a good chance she, and others just like her, will help before and after the surgery and make all that seem easy too. She'd even, for just a short time, eased the lonely ache that never seemed to leave me.

A final thought meandered through my fatigue-blurred brain just before I drifted off to sleep – although Bob had gone on ahead, and our children were scattered far and wide, perhaps I wasn't really alone after all.

'They shall grow not old,
as we that are left grow old;
Age shall not weary them,
nor the years condemn.
At the going down of the sun
and in the morning
We will remember them.'

From *For the Fallen*, by Laurence Binyon

Silence

I try to avoid silence. I go out of my way to do so. I've slept with the radio on these past fifty years, much to my Margie's disgruntlement. Until I reminded her how badly I sleep in silence.

She argued more than once that I should fill social silences with conversation, then she'd laugh at her own twisted humour. She knew me better than anyone. She knew I wasn't one to say much. I miss her now. I hope she knew how much I loved her, how much her sticking by me meant. I tried to show her, even if I couldn't say the words. She knew. Surely.

About the only time I let silence catch up with me is April 25th each year. They say war is about sacrifice. Well, to me, remembering World War 1 in silence is a sacrifice. Because the silence of today echoes with the unavoidable, horrific silence of all those years ago. Let me try to explain...

I grew up the middle lad of five. We worked a spread of Murray Mallee land just out of Pinnaroo. Until the war, Dad always said he was glad he had sons, because it took all of us working hard to keep the place running. When war came, he was proud to manage without my two older brothers, so they could go and fight for freedom.

I was only seventeen, too young to fight. I appreciated silence back then, riding out across the hushed plains, checking sheep and dreaming of my own spread, and settling down with Margie.

As soon as I was eighteen, Dad signed the papers and I was off. Me and my two best mates, Paddy O'Leary and Bobby Bailey, heading off to war to become men. The silence of the farm seemed a long way away with calls of 'best wishes' bouncing around the train station from the gathered townsfolk. Mums and girlfriends gathered together, sobbing quietly, helping one another be brave. My Margie wore a courageous smile. She'd promised to wait for me, which didn't make it any easier to leave her.

Although Broadmeadow was probably closer, we took the train to Adelaide. There was nothing quiet about our new home, Morphettville Camp, with excited soldiers getting to know each other and learning the craft of war. Street parades were even noisier, with rowdy soldiers in brand-new uniforms, full of expectation, cheered on by crowds full of national pride.

Months later at Outer Harbor, there was more cheering from the crowd. Already, we were heroes, just for going. They'd read the papers, heard the stories, knew war was no party. You could see it in the shadow behind their patriotic eyes. They wondered how many of us they'd never see again. I was glad my family hadn't made the trip from Pinnaroo. Without their sad eyes and forced smiles, I could cling to my sense of duty and pretend I was off on the biggest adventure of my life. Off with old mates and new ones, to explore the world on a cruise that would take me places I'd never even heard of.

When the crowd disappeared, the chaplain gathered us all on deck to pray a blessing over our journey. He prayed for victory. He prayed for courage. He prayed for our safe return. After he said 'Amen,' there was silence, and the seed of hatred for it was planted deep in my soul. The hubbub of the crowd that had kept our courage buoyant, kept our sense of duty and integrity strong beneath us disappeared, and we sank into the silence of fear. Fear of all the unknowns before us. Fear that this might be the last time we saw Australia. Fear our mates might know we were afraid. This wouldn't do. I cleared my throat and started on the Lord's Prayer, more to break the silence than anything.

There is no way I can tell you the horror that is war. It is unspeakable. You had to be there, and I wouldn't wish that on anyone. Not even Eugene Michaels, the bully of fourth grade who'd conned my dad into letting him have the pick of our kelpie's litter, only to hang the helpless puppy from a rafter in the shed. And hold me down to watch. I hated him. His vicious streak might have made him a great soldier, but he wasn't in this battle. He had something wrong with his eyes and couldn't come. The whole town had felt sorry for him. He was doubly sorry for himself, having to miss the adventure. None of us knew the truth.

I hated silence more each time I heard it, every night spent in muddy trenches all over France. Not so much for the silence, but for the noises that surrounded it. As night fell, the unthinkable sounds of battle hushed. I hated the noise of war. The explosions. The gunfire. The yelling from our troops and theirs.

Then with darkness came the quiet. And the cold. That first night, I sighed with relief. No more shooting. No more killing. No more war until the new light of tomorrow. It was like every man alive held his soundless breath. But then the cacophony of horror began. The groaning, the wailing of our wounded troops and theirs. The painfilled cries of 'stretcher bearer' springing up from no man's land. The shuffle of soldiers heading out to retrieve their fallen mates. The scurry of rats, heading out to retrieve their dinner.

Even worse, the second silence of the night, when the moaning stopped and Paddy wasn't beside me. I'd lost track of my best mate, hadn't seen him fall. So many were still out there in the night, surrounded by the silence of death. Gone forever for the glory of war.

Months after Paddy was gone, it was my turn to lie silent between our trenches and theirs, surrounded by the lifeless, soundless bodies of dozens from my company. The pain and fire coming from my leg pinned me to the ground. I thought of calling for a stretcher-bearer, but the words just wouldn't come. The darkness closed over me from within, numbing the pain. Was this the silent darkness of death? My last thought... of my sweet Margie.

But I wasn't done with life just yet, it seemed. And silence was nowhere to be found in the hospital, kept away by moans of pain from tough Aussie diggers, screams from soldiers wild with demons fresh from battle, the hum of nurses full of compassion, the sobs of men broken in body and spirit. And I joined the orchestra of agony when they told me I'd left my leg in the mud of the Somme.

For weeks, I wished I'd followed Paddy to the Great Beyond. Death would have been better than this. This agony, this loss, this disability. They told me I was lucky to be alive, lucky to be going home. I should have been more grateful, I suppose. But lying in the hospital at night, far from my mates who fought on, far from Paddy's lonely grave, far from my Margie, the silence of deep sadness engulfed me and took me again to the front.

Others had nightmares too, I guessed by the sudden screams punctuating the night. Nurses soothed brows, offered pain relief with sips of water, reread letters from home, then slipped away softly to avoid disturbing our hard-earned, short-lived peace.

The trip home was nothing like the journey off to war. We'd been young, with barely a thought for what we faced, brave enough to go regardless, into unknown danger. We did it out of duty for our country, and for freedom. We'd grown up overseas, men together against all odds, full of courage and integrity, with a touch of Aussie larrikin thrown in to keep us humble. Coming home, we were broken. We'd never be the same. We'd shared something no one else could ever comprehend. That would bind us together.

As Outer Harbor came into view, the chaplain gathered us all on deck to pray. He'd been with us all the way. He understood. Because he prayed for patience and compassion from and for our families. He prayed for victory over our demons. He prayed for courage. After he said 'Amen,' there was silence and the seed of hatred for it grew deeper in my soul. We'd left so many behind, some alive and fighting on with courage and resilience, others buried in the frozen soil. It was those faces that loomed before me in the silence, Paddy, Bobby and the rest. We stood in fear-filled silence, afraid of all the unknowns before us. Afraid they'd pity our brokenness. Afraid of not knowing how life worked anymore, with us so altered by the battle. This wouldn't do. I cleared my throat and started singing *Keep the Home Fires Burning*, more to break the silence than anything.

I didn't expect a welcome as they wheeled me down the plank. It was too far to come from Pinnaroo. My composure was fragile just being on Aussie soil again, and then I saw them – Dad and

Mum and precious Margie. If I wasn't sitting down, I would have crumpled. So much for being a tough returning soldier, brought down by three loved ones from home. Happy sounds engulfed us, shouts of recognition, cries of reunion and squeals of joy. Despite the rowdy chatter, I could see the silence in my Margie's face. It filled her eyes and spilled over down her cheeks. She knelt beside my wheelchair.

'Thanks for coming all this way,' I muttered.

'Same to you,' she chuckled softly, 'you've come a long way more than me.'

All the way home in the train, they told farm stories, town stories, even district stories, filling in the pieces of what used to be my life. But none of it mattered.

Slowly, ever so slowly, I settled back into post-war life. I settled for life without a leg. I settled for life without Paddy or Bobby. I settled for sleepless, haunted nights. It was by no means all bad, but there were times when it took all the courage and resilience I'd acquired at the front to face another day.

Like the day I sat my Margie down and told her I wouldn't hold her to her promise. She laughed, until I didn't, then she up and slapped me, right across the face. She slapped a hero in a wheelchair. Still, I turned and wheeled away. She chased me down.

'You left more than your leg on the battlefront, Arthur Cooke. You left your senses there as well, if you think a little thing like a wheelchair is going to keep me from marrying you.'

We hollered back and forth for a while, both as stubborn as each other. Then we talked more calmly. Soon after, we were married.

...Between my Margie and our children, and then our grandchildren, I didn't have to face the silence again. And of course, there was the all-night radio. But every ANZAC Day, I attend the Pinnaroo Dawn Service, in remembrance of my fallen mates. I brace myself, and endure the minute's silence in their honour. Their faces still loom there in the silence, like it was yesterday we headed off on that gruesome adventure. In the silence, I remember the suffering, the horror, the death. I remember the heroes, the duty, the courage. I remember my mates, Paddy and Bobby and the rest.

I feel the tension rising within me as the silence lingers longer. Then, just before the bugle breaks it, I hear the song of morning birds. I hear a baby cry, a restless child asking, 'How much longer?'

I hear the sounds of life. In commemoration and reflection, there is life. That's what we fought for.

It was worth it.

With age comes... love

There's plenty of loving going on in the senior years.

People who've lived a long time grow to love
things that are familiar,
like their favourite chair, their routine.

They will very often deeply love their family,
although they may not be accustomed to showing it
the way younger people do.
It might even seem like they are too self-absorbed
to care about anyone but themselves, but, rest assured,they care.
It's just that every little part of life is that much harder when
you finish our book title in the first column, that just getting
through the day takes all the time
and energy they have.

Some seniors will have the privilege of living with
and loving the same person for fifty or sixty years,
long after the honeymoon is over –
there's a lot we can learn about patience, self-sacrifice
and abiding love from them.

Many will have faced the loss of that special person who shared
their home, their bed, their family, their lives.
Never underestimate the effort it takes to carry on alone.

And some will be blessed to find love in their twilight years.

Young Love

Ron slumped into his well-worn recliner, relieved that something old and familiar was still a part of his life. This new place was nice enough, but it didn't feel like home. Before long he drifted off to sleep, even though it was only mid-afternoon. His dreams took him to his happy place, the home he'd shared with Joyce for sixty-two years.

He awoke, dazed by the silence, missing her delightful chatter about this and that and nothing much. Reaching for the remote, he banished the hush with televised nonsense, wishing it could fill the Joyce-shaped hole in his heart.

He missed her. He missed his mates at the club. He missed his neighbours. He missed his vegie patch. He missed the warm nights and warmer days of northern New South Wales. He missed having something, anything, to look forward to.

Ron's fight against the longings would have been easier if he had anything, any little thing, to fill his life here. His son, Eric, had wanted him closer. It didn't seem to matter that he had a comfortable life of his own in the beautiful New England region. Eric said family was more important, and, of course, it was.

Long-distant memories of camping in the Tablelands when the kids were young, trekking all over the district with them for football games on Saturdays and teaching young Eric and his brother Ben how to burn snags on the barbie after church on Sundays flooded Ron's mind. His own dad had always been too busy for such things. His concept of family time was working the farm together, so Ron had grown up determined to both work and play with his kids.

He must have done something right, because they always seemed to enjoy getting together as a family. Even when they grew up and moved away, they'd always come home for Christmas. And, of course, there was their Queen's Birthday long weekend tradition. Every year they rented a huge house in Dubbo and, regardless of what was going on with work or babies or anything, everyone came.

Ron remembered introducing grandchildren and, later, great-grandchildren, to the Dubbo Zoo experience. When it got too hard for Ron and Joyce to be there, the family kept up the tradition without them. Even when Ben settled overseas, the Fergusson family booking remained in place, with June coming up from Tassie with her family, and as many of Carol's kids coming from WA as could make it. Because 'family is important'.

The mantra he'd lived by had turned around and stabbed Ron in the back. With his siblings spread far and wide, Eric had appointed himself in charge of his parents. He'd taken Joyce to all her medical appointments. He'd arranged for in-home care. He'd slept over for a week after she passed.

So when he got promoted and had to move to South Australia, he insisted on Ron moving too. Day after day they sorted and sold, discarded and donated, and finally boxed up what was left of a lifetime's worth of stuff to take with him. Ron bought a unit in a retirement village in a seaside town half an hour from where Eric would be based. It looked lovely online.

But it wasn't home.

Three months later, it still wasn't home, and Eric was gone.

The job didn't work out, and Eric reluctantly returned to New South Wales, minus his dad. Ron had already said goodbye to so many dear friends. He'd parted with so many treasures. The place he'd forever think of as home belonged to someone else now. He'd endured all the paperwork involved in moving states, changing banks and doctors and home care providers, finding a new podiatrist, a new denture clinic, a new hearing aid place. He was physically and emotionally exhausted and simply couldn't handle another move.

So here he was. Alone.

Except for the promise of visits from grandchildren passing through from one place to another. They'd likely stay for coffee, or maybe overnight sometimes, if Ron ever got the spare room set up. Eric would be back on business and hoped to stay for the weekend once a month.

But mostly, it was just him and the wretched television. There'd been a welcoming committee of neighbours from Ron's cul-de-sac. Armed with casserole and cake, they'd dropped in after his first night, bombarding him with questions and information. Fortunately, most of what they'd said was documented in the village newsletter, so he knew exactly when the Scrabble tournament was held, what afternoon Bingo was played, and where to find the men's shed.

Not that he'd had the energy or inclination for any of those things. Not yet. He'd been flat out unpacking and settling in, in between meeting his new carers, his new doctor, and his new minister.

Something caught his eye outside. An unfamiliar car pulled in to Number 32 across the way. After three months, he thought he knew all the cars belonging in his cul-de-sac. He'd never seen any cars, nor any people, at Number 32. Until now. And they weren't visiting, because the roller door was going up.

Easing out of his recliner, Ron approached the window, gently parting the curtain for a better look. A woman got out of the car and walked toward the letter box. Although there's no way he could have known her, something about her looked familiar. She looked up from her mail. Ron dropped the curtain and stepped back from the window, but it was too late. Looking straight at him, she waved, a cheeky smile brightening her face.

A smile Ron knew he'd seen before. If he could only remember when.

He pondered the issue as he microwaved his Meals-on-Wheels soup, as he sliced cheese for the toast he'd dunk into it because Joyce wasn't there to tell him off, and was no closer to an answer when he prepared for bed, hoping the sleeping pill the doctor had given him would work this time.

It did more than work. It filled his slumber with dreams, of Joyce, their home, their special times together. There was nothing unusual about that. The strange, surely drug-induced part of the night was the ever-present, new, but strangely familiar cheeky smile of the lady across the way, leering nightmarishly in every pleasant scene.

Ron awoke confused, distracted, and poorly rested. He'd only just got through his morning routine, slower than usual this morning, when the doorbell rang. It was way too early for Meals-on-Wheels, and there were no carers due today. A glance out the window as he approached the door told him whoever it was hadn't driven, as there were no cars outside his place.

He opened the door and was greeted with a cheery, 'Welcome to Sunny Gardens', as a plate of Anzac biscuits was thrust toward his chest. 'Sorry I wasn't here to welcome you. You arrived while I was visiting my daughter interstate. I spend most winters with her, away from this bone-chilling cold. Have you noticed how cold it is here? Perhaps you don't notice it. You may well be used to it, I suppose, if you come from down this way. When did you move in? Do you come from around here? Is your wife at home? Shall I put these in the kitchen? I hope you like Anzacs. They're completely free of nuts, in case you're allergic, but they're not gluten-free, sorry. If you are, that is. Gluten-free, I mean.'

Ron just stood in the doorway, somewhat dazed by the avalanche of words. He knew he should take the plate of biscuits, and smile his thanks. It would be polite, even neighbourly, to attempt to answer some of her questions, but she'd fired them off so fast he wasn't sure where to start.

As much as he wanted to blame her and her non-stop gabbing for his appalling manners, he knew it was more to do with her eyes. Something about them simply took his breath away, making it impossible for him to put two cohesive words together.

Although he'd never met this un-named woman before, he was convinced he'd seen those deep green eyes twinkling at him before. And they had him mesmerized.

Ron forced himself to look away and realised she was talking still, '...like it here. Have you made friends with anyone yet? Ken from Number 29 is a lovely man, particularly if you like gardening.'

Sensible words began to coalesce in his head, finally, and he opened his mouth to let them out. It hung open and stayed that way long enough to catch flies if only the weather had been warmer when she said, 'How rude of me, I've stood here prattling on all this time without introducing myself. I'm Ruth Pritchard, from Number 32 across the way.'

Ron felt a penny drop in the back of his mind, but with inflation, and the advent of decimal currency, he knew he'd need more than a single penny to put the pieces together.

'Nice to meet you, Ruth. Thanks for the biscuits.' Glad his manners had finally decided to show up and take over from his blithering self, he reached for the plate and drew it towards him. 'Anzacs are my favourite. I'd invite you in, but I'm afraid now isn't a good time. If you'll excuse me.' With that, he began closing the door, hoping she wouldn't take offence. Well, not too much, at least.

Hiding behind his curtain once again, Ron studied her retreating form. A fine looking woman. And a fine cook too, if the aroma wafting from the plate as he lifted the Gladwrap was anything to go by.

He almost heard the ka-ching of another penny dropping as his teeth sunk into that first Anzac – crunchy on the outside, chewy in the middle, just the way he preferred them. Joyce had liked hers crunchy all the way through, and that's how hers always turned out, and he never complained. The taste was the same. Still, he'd had them just like this before, somewhere.

He couldn't remember what he'd had planned for the rest of the day, but was drawn to the shelf in the linen cupboard set aside for photos. An old bloke on his own didn't have much linen, so he was using the space for general storage. He dug in under numerous albums full of family photos, until, deeper still beneath their wedding album, he found what he hadn't realised he was looking for – a shoebox full of images from his own childhood and youth.

And there they were. A whole bank-load of pennies dropped when he saw those sparkling deep-green eyes staring at him from a much younger, wrinkle-free face, along with that familiar cheeky smile.

Had photography been as easy then as it was today for those who could master digital technology and fang-dangled phones better than Ron could, there would have been more than the single photo of eighteen-year-old Ruth Thompson standing beside tuxedoed Ron Fergusson at the Quirindi Debutante Ball of 1954. There for sure would have been photos of them winning the three-legged race at the church spring picnic when he was ten and she was eight. And more of them singing together in the school choir, playing on the rope swing out across the swollen creek the year the big rains came, and trying to catch a summer breeze by camping out in the top paddock.

He and Ruth had been rivals, teammates, confidantes, partners in crime, best friends. They'd been inseparable. Until her family moved away from the area so her older brothers could go to university in the city. They'd written a few times, but city life was busy for Ruth, and it wasn't long before Ron met Joyce.

Fancy her turning up now, and living right across the cul-de-sac. Ron wondered if there was a Mr Pritchard sitting in Number

32 right now, munching on perfect Anzac biscuits. He hoped so, and that they'd been happy. That she'd been well-loved and provided for as she deserved. That they might all become friends.

He watched from behind his curtain for a week, pretending not to be home when she rang his doorbell. All four times. Always alone. And he hurried away on his gopher with a wave even though he could see her approaching with that smile, once again on her own.

For the entire week, there was no sign of Mr Pritchard. She came and went often, but always solo.

After a particularly exhausting day of sleuthing and avoidance, Ron gave himself a strict talking to as he ate the final Anzac, reminding himself that he was, well and truly, a grown-up. So what if there was a Mr Pritchard. He could still make his identity known to Ruth and carry on as polite friends. He'd visit tomorrow. There was a plate to return, after all. And a photo to reveal. He hoped she didn't have memory issues, or that what they'd shared had meant nothing to her. Because, more than anything, Ron found himself desperately wanting Ruth to remember him.

The next morning, Ruth answered his knock quickly, almost as though she'd been expecting him. Her green eyes sparkled and the delicious aroma of more Anzacs, if Ron's nose wasn't mistaken, greeted him when she opened the door.

'Why, hello Ron, would you like to come in? I usually have a cuppa about now. Perhaps you'd care to join me.'

Ron noted the singular pronouns, strongly suggestive that there was no Mr Pritchard. Unless, of course, he was out. Perhaps he'd found his way to the men's shed while Ron was busy with his carer. Ron decided he needed to take the direct approach.

'That sounds delightful, but perhaps we should wait for your husband?'

'I was widowed ten years ago, Ron, after forty-seven wonderful years. Come on in. How do you take your tea? Or would you rather coffee?'

'I'll have tea, thanks. White with one sugar.' Ron followed her into the house, pulling his shoulders back and inhaling deeply, drawing in air like it was courage. It must have helped, because all of a sudden he heard himself blurting, 'Unless, of course, you have cocoa and marshmallows, like we used to drink around those campfires in the top paddock?'

Ruth stopped in her tracks, oddly silent. She turned. Those eyes, less sparkly now and more inquisitive, roamed his face, her smile more puzzled than cheeky.

'Ron?'

'Ruth.'

'Ron Fergusson from the Nundle district of New England, New South Wales?'

'The very one, Ruth Thompson. Fancy meeting you, here, right across the cul-de-sac from me, after all these years.'

'Fancy indeed! How long have you known? How did you work it out? You've changed, Ron. Lost some hair, gained some weight, and some wrinkles...' Ron tuned out the rest, captivated by the woman standing before him, who hadn't changed a bit. She was still chatty and upbeat, full of questions, full of life.

Ron looked forward to hearing all about her life, and telling her all about his. He wanted to tell her how happy he'd been with Joyce. They'd have to share a lot of cups of tea, a lot of mornings, afternoons and, perhaps evenings too, if they hoped to cover two lifetimes full of laughter and tears, memories and photos. And hopefully many, many more of those perfect Anzac biscuits to fuel their conversations.

It seemed, finally, Ron had something to look forward to.

'You don't stop laughing when you grow old,
you grow old when you stop laughing.'

George Bernard Shaw

The Last One Left

'Well, that's another one over and done with.'

'Grampa,' Joshua's raised brows and wide eyes express his horror more than his words do. 'That's a terrible thing to say about Mr Bennett. I thought he was one of your friends?'

'Ha! My dear boy. I wasn't referring to the life being over and done with. I meant the funeral. I seem to be going to a good many of them lately. In fact, I would venture to say that the only time I get out of 'The Home' is for doctor's appointments and funerals.'

The walk from the church to the car park is a short one. However, I'm not quite done talking yet. I continue my funeral rant as Joshua helps me into his car.

'Mind you, I am, at least, choosey about the ones I go to. A silly old lady down the hall from me combs through the papers and goes to one nearly every day. Doesn't even know half the deceased. Just goes for the outing. And the afternoon tea. Nothing wrong with the afternoon tea they serve us at 'The Home', in my opinion.

'I have to share a table with her in the dining room. Set seating, you know. And every meal she's on about whichever funeral she's just been to. As much as I hate eating alone, the way she drones on is just plain irritating.'

'Well, Grampa, I guess she's just a lonely soul who's pleased to have a handsome gentleman to share her table and some conversation with.'

'Yes. Yes, Joshua. I know. And I should be more gracious.' The chagrin I feel at his gentle scolding holds my tongue as he navigates through city traffic.

'Is there anywhere else you'd like to go while we're out, Grampa?'

'If you have time, it would be nice to visit Lake Shore Park. There's a bench there I love to sit on, and the weather is just about perfect.'

Joshua makes the necessary adjustments to his course, and we head for the park. He's a good lad, this grandson of mine. They all are. I have a wonderful, supportive family. Any time I need to go somewhere, one of them is there to take me. I secretly wonder whether they draw straws – short straw has to take 'The Old Boy' out!

Even though Joshua is mindful to park as close as he can, I'm still huffing when my feet feel the grass of my favourite park beneath them. Still, the closest bench won't do. I shake my head at Joshua's silent enquiry, and stride out to the third bench, facing the lake.

'What's so special about this one, Grampa?'

'I love to sit here and reflect on all the wonderful times I've had in my life. I courted your Gramma on this bench. We spent hours talking, laughing, getting to know everything about each other.' My voice gets lost in the myriad of memories, and I stare out over the water for what seems like forever. 'Sometimes she brought old bread and we'd feed the ducks. Ha! Such antics they'd display. Like going to a circus, only cheaper.'

'I remember how you and Gramma held hands all the time. And how her eyes sparkled when she looked at you. I hope I'll find a woman to look at me that way. Someone I can love forever.'

'Forever was the way marriages were in our day. Few people seriously considered divorce. We used struggles to make us stronger as a couple. I'm forever thankful that your Gramma stuck by me when I lost my job and very nearly lost the house. And I wouldn't have been anywhere but by her side through her battle with post-natal depression, though they never gave it a name back then.'

'Did you and Gramma ever buy donuts from the cart over there?'

'We sure did. I'll shout if you go get them.'

Between bites of the best hot cinnamon donuts ever, Joshua ventures another question. 'At the funeral today, Grampa, what did those people mean when they came up and shook your hand and said you were the last one left? Was it some sort of club?'

'One of the things about living past ninety, Joshua, is that you outlive everyone. They said it last year at my brother's funeral. I'm the last one left of all my brothers and sisters. There were nine of us, and now there's just me. I even buried those younger than me, starting before you were born when my youngest brother was killed in a tractor accident. Sure thought some of the others would see me out, but I'm the last one left.'

I look out over the lake. 'Even though we were scattered all over the country, we were always there for each other whenever there was a need. Not anymore.'

He seems to respect my need for silence as I lose myself down memory lane for a time.

'Funny how reflection works. I look at the lake and see the sky, the clouds, the trees bouncing back at me like they were real, except for the shimmer and ripple of the water. I look back at my memories and they seem so real, like it was yesterday, except for the fog of time, the distortion of perspective.'

'What do you mean, Grampa?'

'With time and the wisdom that comes with age, some of the things that seemed so important at the time seem so trivial now. I could have laughed more if I knew then what I know now.'

Joshua reached over and brushed sugar off the front of my jacket. Pity. Seeing it there might have made the funeral fanatic back at 'The Home' turn green with envy.

'Too many good memories to begrudge them all leaving me.' Sitting up straighter, I shake off the gloom, then realise there's more. 'People said the same thing at Fred Williamson's funeral five years ago. When he died, I became the only one left of my platoon. Well, the whole company actually. I spent the best and the worst of times with those boys, and there's no one left to share the stories and memories. No one else chuckles at the sound of Bing Crosby and The Andrews Sisters crooning the '*Vict'ry Polka*'. We sang that song for miles in the jeep convoys. And killed it in the showers.'

'Did you keep in touch over the years?'

'You bet. Every Anzac Day as many of us as could would march in the city march, then get together at the RSL Clubrooms. Lots of them drank and played two-up. I was mostly in it for the yarns, the memories, and catching up on how they were all doing. But there got to be less and less as the years went by. Now that I'm the last one left I don't bother going to the march anymore.'

'You know, Grampa, any of us grandkids would be proud to march with you next year.'

'Thanks, Joshua, but no. I was never in it for the glory. It was always about the mateship, and with no mates left, it's just not worth the effort.'

'So, Mr Bennett wasn't an army buddy?'

'No. Billy and I go way further back than that. We were in school together, all the way through. He had to stay home from the war with a weak chest. Wrote to me though, every couple of weeks. We were best man at each other's weddings. Kept up every so often over the years. Life gets busy, you know, once the family comes along. Saw each other at a High School reunion the year we turned fifty. Since then, we've seen each other pretty regularly, at funerals. Billy and I have stood together and watched classmate after classmate lowered into the ground. Until today of course. That's why his family said I was the last one left.' My eyes follow my memories into the far distance, and I stare over the lake as my mind relives all those far-away moments.

Enough!

I realise with a start that I should be living in this moment, making a memory right now with Joshua, rather than replaying old ones.

'How about a cup of hot chips, Joshua?'

'I thought you said the food was good at 'The Home.' Seems to me like they don't feed you enough.'

'No, it's just that food tastes better on a park bench, with family for company and a lake to look out over.'

'How about if you come up with some more stories while I get the chips.'

Just as well he brings steaming coffees too. All the chatting is enough to dry a body's pipes something shocking.

'I hope my questions didn't make you miserable before, Grampa. You don't have to tell me more stories if it depresses you. But you know, I do love listening to your stories.'

'No, Sonny, the memories don't make me sad. I've had a wonderful life, filled with great friends and a very loving family. Remembering the good things helps me forget the bad about myself, the poor choices I made at times, and the weaknesses I've seen in other people. I'll be happy to tell you some more funeral stories. Believe me, I've got plenty more.

'I remember going to a funeral a couple of months ago. Fred Foster. He was the school bully and rumour was that his Dad lay into him and his Mum, and anyone who tried to interfere. Instead of trying to overcome his Dad's example, Fred followed it. Somehow he managed to get himself a wife and some kids, but none of them were ever happy. Hate perpetuates itself, Joshua, unless you stand against it.'

'So, was there anyone at the funeral, other than you? Why did you bother going?'

'I mainly went to support his wife, Joyleen, and make sure someone would keep an eye on her. It was just me, her, their children and their families. I remember shaking hands with the celebrant after the very short service and congratulating him on doing a good job under difficult circumstances. With a knowing look, he commented that I must know the family pretty well. Easing up close so no one else would hear, I said I knew them well enough to know that the little good he'd managed to say was fabricated. Every kind word was a load of garbage: all lies. But then, it's not proper to speak ill of the dead.'

'That's horrible, Grampa. It sure makes me think about my own life. I want to live the kind of life that will allow people to speak well of me at my funeral, without having to make things up or lie or exaggerate. I want everyone at my funeral to be able to share good memories and tell stories of what a great person I was.'

'Well, Joshua, you have just become one of the few good things that came out of the life and death of Fred Foster.'

'You mean there were others?'

'He had four kids. The oldest boy ran away from home as soon as he could get a job. He seems to have broken the abuse cycle and was treating his wife and children well at the service. He assured me he'd be taking care of his mum now. I felt sorry for one of the girls, though. She looked as though she didn't think much of herself, and didn't expect others to either.'

'Wow, Grampa, you sound like a social worker. Did you do studies on all this stuff?'

'Ha! No Joshua, my boy. Life is the best teacher of all. So I've been 'studying' for over ninety years now. I know a lot about human nature and how people think, just by rubbing shoulders with them for so long. We old people call it the 'wisdom of experience'. When I was young, my generation had a great deal of respect for those with the wisdom of experience. I'm not sure it's the 'in' thing now-a-days. Your generation seems to like to work life out for themselves. Make your own mistakes. That's fair enough, but it's hard for us oldies to sit by and watch you start over and make all the same mistakes we did.'

I've been talking way too long. I take a sip of the now cold coffee and once again find myself mesmerised by the lake, especially when a group of children rode by on their bikes, frightening a flock of ducks into flight. Their departure stirred up the surface of the water.

'You know, Joshua, a funeral is like this lake – it offers a reflection of a life. I hope there are not too many ripples at my funeral.'

'What do you mean, Grampa?'

'Well, I hope you won't need to distort the memories to make my life sound better.'

'What foolishness, Grampa. Of course we'll speak well of you. You always have a kind word and a smile. You're the happiest old man I know. We'll most likely be sharing your jokes at your funeral, and trying to out-do each other with funny stories. In between the tears, that is.'

'No tears. I want a happy funeral. A celebration of a long and happy life. And you'd better make it a good afternoon tea too, because my funeral fanatic friend is bound to be there.'

'We will Grampa. But it's starting to get cold, now. I'd better take you back to 'The Home'. You know you really should write down your stories and thoughts. Not just so we can read them out at your funeral, but so that my future kids can learn from your wisdom, like I have.'

'You mean write my own eulogy?'

'Exactly. That's the only way you'll get it just the way you want it.'

'Ha! Maybe I'll do just that.'

'He who is of a calm and happy nature will hardly feel
the pressure of age,
but to him who is of an opposite disposition,
youth and age are equally a burden.'

Plato

A Peaceful Getaway

All I really wanted was to get away for a while before I settle into the retirement that has been thrust upon me way before I felt ready. I may be well into my sixties, but I still feel competent, capable, and proficient. Although I consider myself to be well able to fulfil my duties, the powers that be deemed me 'too old' to work in the ER, where I'd helped thousands of patients, and seen many younger nurses come and go over the years. They didn't even offer me a transfer to a safer, quieter department. Just a thankless golden handshake.

So, I decided to leave without a fuss before I wanted to, and take their not-so-generous bribe and see somewhere new. Somewhere no one would know me. Or need me.

Because, and I would never admit it to them, being needed so much had, in reality, been tough just lately. Nothing a good holiday wouldn't fix, though. I'm used to being tired after a shift in the regional ER where I worked, but recently, it had been more than tired. I'd started to get discouraged, cynical and just plain disillusioned with the state of humankind.

I'm accustomed to strange cases, weird situations, and wacky presentations, but people generally used to appreciate being helped. They were decent, kind, civilised. But over the last little while, with so many drugs on the streets, so much domestic violence, so much yuck everywhere, it had all been getting more traumatic, more weird. Most tiring of all was having to be nice to people.

Even when they weren't nice to me.

It's more than work, though, that's left me feeling tired before I start each new day. And it's nothing to do with getting old. It's more because I find myself consumed with anxiety of late. What sort of world will my grandchildren grow up in? Will they forget how to carry on a conversation; or how to share their feelings without an emoji; or how to be a friend to someone special by being there for them, instead of just liking a post?

In case you haven't noticed, my pet hate is technology. I can see its benefits, but I worry about its influence on my grandies. It's sometimes hard to remember that I'm only the grandma. I get to watch them play their sport, and perform in all manner of concerts, but it's not my place to set the rules or fix what no one else thinks is broken. Still, whilst driving long distances to be part of their busy lives, I worry, and hope they put their phones away every so often and immerse themselves fully in their social activities.

Don't get me wrong – I adore my grandchildren, and would do anything for them. I love being a part of their lives. It's just, well, their lives are so busy and the effort to know them sometimes wears me out.

And then there's my husband. Someone else I worry about. You've heard of the absent-minded professor? I married him. Not that he was a professor when I married him. Or absent-minded. That I'd noticed, anyway. He became well-respected in the academic world. A sought-after conference speaker. Up to his eyeballs in research grants, book offers and journal articles, even well-and-truly after he entered retirement age. Pity those eye-balls so rarely benefitted from the personalised ophthalmic aides he paid so much for.

Unless I'm there to find his glasses for him. And his keys. And the iPad with his lecture notes. And the flash drive with his conference PowerPoint. When his tie doesn't match his shirt, conference attendees chuckle amongst themselves saying, 'All the best academics are a little eccentric.' Only his assistant guesses I was at work when he left the house and races to check whether he has everything else he'll need.

And calls me when it isn't there.

He's always been that way, though, so I'm certain it's distraction rather than dementia, for which I'm forever grateful. Distraction is cute, funny, forgivable and overcomable with effort. Dementia is a horrible disease and I wouldn't wish it on anyone, especially for their family's sake.

To keep my sanity, and to have the much-obsessed over and highly recommended, but mostly overrated, 'me-time', I meet for coffee once a fortnight with as many of the half-dozen girlfriends as can make it. To talk about the book we've been reading.

Or not.

By that I mean that, half the time, I haven't found the time to read said book. And the other half, usually when I have read more than half a page on the loo, they talk about a major drama in someone's life instead. Naturally, great-aunt Flo's tragic illness, the neighbour-two-doors-down's near divorce or the death of the axolotl belonging to Sally's cousin-twice-removed were significant events. But not as relaxing as talking about the book.

Which I'd read.

Now you know why I want, no, need to get away for a while. See somewhere new. Somewhere no one will know me. Or need me.

My therapist insisted on it. I booked it to miss the least number of grandchildren events and waved to my husband as I drove away, mumbling a 'Good luck to one and all,' under my breath. It was all I could say, for fear that worrying about everything and all that could go wrong without me would nullify any possible therapeutic benefits from the trip.

And ruin a good holiday.

I was on my way to a peaceful island getaway. No cars were allowed on Rottnest Island. Sounded like heaven to me. No rushing, no traffic, no last-minute dashes with the eye-wear. I could do whatever I felt like, whenever I felt like it. Like water surrounded the island, isolating it from the mainland, I would be surrounded by strangers, isolated from their needs by anonymity.

Waking up for the third day on the train, itself an island floating across a sea of barren outback, I let its rhythmic rattle and sway soothe the ache in my soul. I felt younger and less anxious with each passing kilometre, and although I savoured my aloneness, I did miss my family. Wondered how they were doing. Hoped they were missing me.

I was glad I'd chosen to journey west by train and brought some good fiction with me. I was halfway through my second book, loving being able to fully immerse myself in the lives and loves of the characters. So much more satisfying than snatching snippets here and there. Together with the mind-numbing boredom of a luxurious, but very long trip, reading had helped me relax.

I spent several hours glancing up periodically from my romantic adventure in the Greek Islands, only to see nothing had changed out the window, because there was nothing out there but flat red dusty plains. I was so ready to explore the golden beaches and lush green parks on the island. I craved colour and freshness and water.

An explosion shattered my reverie. With a jolt, the train came to a sudden and screeching stop. Chaos erupted around me. Out the window, a wreckers' yard worth of metal flew past in various sizes, some dangerously large and fast.

Like an earthquake, a second explosion, much closer and louder, rocked the carriage I was in. Thunderous metal hailstones pelted the roof, denting it, threatening to bring it down on top of us. Above the cacophony of metal sounds, I heard a sound that never failed to awaken every cell within me, ready for action – the sound of human screaming.

I hesitated, unsure whether to stay in the doubtful shelter of the carriage that threatened collapse, or risk being flattened by flying debris. A third explosion, this one towards the rear of the train, ended my indecision, and I ran from the train.

It wasn't flying wreckage that hit me first, it was hot air. We were in the desert, after all. And it was February. Heat from fires at both ends of the train only added to the scorching temperatures. I wrapped my silk scarf, adorned with pale pink frangipani, a gift to commemorate our anniversary, over my nose and mouth, hoping to keep the soot and smoke out of my lungs.

I was unsure where to start. I needed to find a safe place for triage. I needed to collect any available first aid supplies. I needed a railway official to tell me what on earth had gone wrong. I needed phone reception to call for help. I needed the 'Mass Casualties

Manual' from the ER nurse's station. The red folder on the top shelf. The one with the emergency protocol for major disasters. I needed help. I needed…a moment.

In that moment, I realised there was no phone reception. And no hill to climb and stand on one leg with my hand in the air to find reception like they always did in the movies. No railway staff had survived to enlighten me. Not even a cleaner.

I closed my eyes. Inhaled deeply through the pink frangipani scarf. Exhaled slowly. And again. In…Out.

Then instinct kicked in. And with it, a calm authority I didn't recognise as my own. I was needed and so, regardless of what people thought were the limitations of my age, I could do this. Despite the heat; the symphony of cries for help, some loud and desperate, others soft and low and likely more urgent; and the taste of burning diesel in the air, I took charge.

And everybody let me.

Those with able bodies helped the wounded. They were brought to me. Someone found a geriatric nurse – in both nature and speciality. But she knew a crisis when she saw one, and pitched right in, following my directions with enthusiasm.

They brought me burn victims, people with lacerations caused by flying debris and people with bones broken as the force of the explosion upended carriages like a cat let loose in a model railway museum. Smoke and flying ashes exacerbated asthma and stung eyes. Stress triggered angina. The lack of lunch sent blood sugar levels plummeting in those with diabetes.

A brave scavenger re-entered the train, collecting bedding from the sleeping berths to tear up for bandages. He proudly brought load after load of loot to me – two first-aid kits, a bucket of water, a soap dispenser he'd levered off the wall. I quickly fell in love with this guy – my very own, and only, supply department. His gifts were gold.

There wasn't time to comb through the highly damaged sections of the train – we had a steady flow of patients without risking more lives in the burning front end, the fractured centre carriages, or the disintegrating rear portion, where the third explosion had occurred.

The scorching mid-day sun was relentless, with no trees for shade, and not a cloud in sight. It wasn't long before my ingenious life-saver, the requisitions officer, rigged up a shelter from train curtains. The wounded were efficiently moved into the shade, groaning as the disturbance heightened their pain.

I worked on auto-pilot, oblivious to the weariness, the aches, and the hunger my adrenaline suppressed, suturing lacerated arteries with needle and thread from a sewing kit, setting fractured limbs, giving orders willingly obeyed.

Hours must have passed in the frenzy, and suddenly, we had other problems. I'd been too focussed on the urgent to think of the important. Like our need for rescue, our need for food, and the inevitable approach of nightfall. I was completely ignorant of the fact that deserts, though oppressively hot during the day, can reach dangerously low temperatures overnight.

Lucky for me my scavenger knew about desert survival. There wasn't much he could pull out and burn – it was mostly metal and plastic, but he'd found blankets.

In the last of the daylight, with all the injured we'd located as comfortable as possible, I gathered a search and rescue team and headed for the most damaged carriages. Horror awaited us. Severed limbs, spilt blood, unrecognisable body parts fused by inconceivable temperatures to grotesquely disfigured parts of the train.

What had happened was beyond my guess. Was this an accident? My recent inclination to cynicism had me suspicious of there being a terrorist amongst us, standing back in the shadows delighting in the destruction they'd inflicted. I had to refuse to travel that path for fear of being paralysed into inactivity by the anger and dread such a scenario would trigger. I couldn't let the possibility stop me.

By the light of several torches and some phone lights, we checked the other two explosion centres. The rear of the train, the galley carriage, was entirely missing, scattered in pieces across the desert around us. From the last remaining carriage, we heard a sob.

Guilt spread through me like maple syrup drizzled over pancakes, soaking into every pore. Had someone lingered, suffering, all these hours while I was busy dealing with less desperate patients? Torch beams followed the sound of sobbing, eventually illuminating a small child, seemingly unharmed, trapped beneath the protective form of her mother, who hadn't made it. An island of life in a sea of death and destruction.

Those with me raised the deceased mother, and I lifted her daughter away, hugging her to me, offering the only thing I had left to give – caring arms. Back at the makeshift hospital, a grieving mother latched onto my little orphan. Together, they wandered into the darkness, comforting one another without words.

I stopped for a moment and looked around. The fires were out. The sky, blackened by the lack of man-made light, was adorned with the brightest stars I'd ever seen. Below, as if in a mirror, black earth was dotted with starrish bursts of torchlight.

It could have been beautiful. If we'd known help was on its way. If we weren't hungry. If night birds composed the soundtrack of the night instead of survivors moaning in agony. But there was no beauty here. Only fear, pain, and need.

And complete and utter exhaustion. Once I stopped, I realised just how much the hours of intensity had taken out of me. I was done in, sapped of all energy and ability. I sunk to the ground where I stood, and snatched moments of sleep between calls for help from the wounded. Dawn came, a welcome relief from the blackness. I wondered how long before the rescue planes reached us.

They came at last, mid-afternoon. I couldn't leave a critical patient to offer a welcome, so they approached me.

'Need some help?' one asked.

'Sure, since you're here,' I said with a beyond-tired smile.

I stayed with the passengers that didn't need to be airlifted, waiting for a train that had been sent to collect us. Surveying the wreckage, I wondered how any of us had survived. Not quite the peaceful getaway I'd planned.

But I had ended up on an island, of sorts. An island in the desert, separated from the mainland by a wide expanse of emptiness, covered in hot desert sand, and ash, and metal fragments that had once been a train.

And I'd been an island, too. An island of help surrounded by a sea of need. Need which hadn't had its usual draining effect, but instead had empowered me to do better, like Popeye's can of spinach in the old cartoon. This time, need urged me on to work harder and longer than I'd ever done before.

I'd been right all along. I was competent and capable. In fact, I'd never felt as alive as I did in that desert, surrounded by death and suffering.

I'd loved being needed. Thrived on it, in fact.

The difference wasn't the situation, it was the appreciation. Here I wasn't the straight-laced 'old duck' putting an end to an addict's high. I wasn't the nuisance nurse asking nosy questions about how a fall down the stairs caused that pattern of bruises. Here my assistance was valued, my knowledge respected, my skills sought-after.

Mind you, I was still worn out. Even after the time it took for the railway team to clear the track ahead of the rescue train, my weary legs could scarcely carry my own weight. A hero's welcome awaited me when we got to the hospital, but my only concern was the well-being of my patients, then finding a hotel for a very long, hot shower, followed by a very long, uninterrupted sleep. And then...

Well, as much as I needed a holiday, I no longer felt any desire to run away to some island getaway where no one would even know me, let alone need me. My only longing was to go home. Home to my absent-minded professor. Home to my busy grandchildren. But I wasn't returning as a washed-up, too-old-to-be-of-any-value nurse who'd been forced into retirement before she was ready. No, I was going home confident in my abilities and content in my choice to take it easy after a fulfilling career, my decision to direct my skills and energy in other directions.

I was going home, where I was needed most.

With age comes... grandchildren

I've recently become a Grandma. What a joy. What an absolute
delight. And what an awesome responsibility.

There seems to be an invisible connection between
my granddaughter and me.
We know each other. I love her more than life itself and would
do anything for her. And yet, she's not my child.

That's where the responsibility comes in – I need to believe I did
my job well when I was raising my own children – that I did the
best I knew how at the time, the best I could manage under
the circumstances. And now it's my daughter's turn.
I need to take a step back, and give her the space to parent
in her own way. I need to trust her to do the best she can.

I'm still going to enjoy every chance I get to sow good seeds into
my granddaughter's life, to laugh and love and teach and play,
and offer the gift of time that's in such short supply
for working mums these days.

And I'll also try to respect that they won't always
do things the way I would have.

That can be tough on a grandparent. Especially when distance
is involved. So when you think about older people, remember
that they are likely always longing for more – more visits,
more information, more time –
all the while struggling to honour your preference for space.

Sharing a Sunrise

Eve couldn't believe what they'd done.

She'd been hoping to get a smart phone for her fifteenth birthday. Reading the note on the birthday card again, she realised she should be more grateful:

'This entitles the birthday girl to two weeks on a riverboat with the entire family.'

She'd lived with her grandparents ever since her Mum ran off four years ago. They only saw her Dad one week in every three, when he came back from the mines. Even when he was off work, he wasn't home with them much. Eve could only guess it was because she and her older sister, Amanda, reminded him of Mum, the love of his life, who ran off to 'find herself' somewhere else.

So, Eve had to live with Granny and Grampa, and put up with their old-fashioned way of doing things. She had to force a smile every day when she used her archaic 'flip' phone, knowing that her friends called it a 'dumb' phone. She watched with envy as Amanda spent hours surfing the net, playing games and keeping in touch with all her friends on her 'smart' phone. She'd get one too, just as soon as she had a job and could afford one, and pay for the phone credit.

Eve snapped out of her regret-riddled reverie, smiled, and moved to hug her grandparents. They said the trip would be in the

October term break. Uncle Stuart and his family were looking forward to joining them, so it would be just like family holidays when Mum was growing up. She forgot sometimes that they were her Mum's family. Maybe a houseboat holiday with them wouldn't be so bad after all.

Disappointment descended again when there wasn't a gift from her Dad. She convinced herself it would come in tomorrow's post.

But deep down she knew that wasn't true.

* * * * *

Eve had been expecting a run-down floating beach shack, and couldn't imagine how she'd survive two weeks without modern conveniences. Of course, she was hardly accustomed to excesses of luxury, with the very sensible lifestyle her grandparents held to, but she did like her long hot showers and her microwaved popcorn. She couldn't believe her eyes when they pulled up next to a huge, sleek, state-of-the-art houseboat, looking like a glamourous hotel on the river.

A gigantic grin erupted on her face as Eve rushed aboard and found a fully outfitted kitchen, complete with microwave; a ginormous spa; a television twice the size of the one they had at home; and a stunning deck, with patio furniture to rival Grampa's favourite recliner.

This might just be a great holiday after all.

Amanda flopped down in one of the deck chairs, hardly aware of her surroundings, busy on her phone. Eve determined to explore without her, hoping to stake her claim on the best bed before Amanda even realised where she was.

Having thoroughly investigated every decadent room, Eve returned to the deck in time to hear Grampa relaying a phone message from her Dad. It hardly surprised her that roster changes meant he couldn't join them. It didn't even really make her feel sad. She'd gotten used to not being able to count on him for anything.

Rather than lose herself in such depressing thoughts, Eve got busy welcoming Uncle Stuart, Aunty Rose, and three energetic cousins, who arrived with lots of luggage, loads of laughs, and heaps of hilarious chatter. She couldn't miss her dad for long with all that going on. Grabbing Mattie's backpack, Eve directed her to the room they would share with Amanda, pleased to see her still too busy on the phone to argue over the top bunk.

* * * * *

Eve awoke the next day, amazed to have slept so well in a strange bed. She and Mattie had chatted for a while before they went to sleep, catching up on each other's lives, giggling over the antics of Mattie's little brothers, and oohing and aahing over news of Mattie's love life.

Sneaking out of their room, Eve followed a tantalizing aroma that led her straight to the kitchen, where Granny was cooking breakfast. She could hardly believe her nose. She could count on one hand the number of cooked breakfasts they'd had since moving in with her grandparents. Eve said so to Granny as she watched her turn the sizzling bacon.

'Holidays are all about spoiling ourselves, after being sensible long enough to afford it,' Granny declared.

Eve heartily agreed, especially when she sipped the freshly brewed coffee.

Her offer to help landed her in charge of the sausages. She lost track of everything and almost forgot to rotate her sputtering charges as she listened to Granny's stories of her growing up years: cooking breakfast every day for her father and brothers, strengthening them for a hard day's work on the farm; walking a mile to school; getting home and doing her share of the chores. It sounded like a hard life, but the twinkle in Granny's eyes revealed it must have been a happy one.

Granny's final comment about those being the good old days, before technology stole the life out of everything, puzzled Eve. But only until the food was ready. Cooking had made her hungry and she was quick to join the noisy crowd in the race to devour it.

After loading the dishwasher – fancy a houseboat having a dishwasher – Eve slathered on the sunscreen and dug around in her stuff for her sunhat. She invited Amanda to go fishing with her and Grampa, receiving only a grunt in reply. Fancy choosing to stay inside playing on her phone, earbuds stealing the sounds of the river whilst continuing to deliver the well-used playlist she always listened to. Eve preferred the challenge of doing new things.

* * * * *

Eve sunk into her soft, cosy bunk that night, completely exhausted yet completely happy. She'd spent a wonderful day with her family, catching two decent-sized fish with Grampa, and lots of little ones that had to go back. She'd come as close as she ever had to beating Aunty Rose at Scrabble. And she'd hiked along the shore with her boisterous cousins: shrieking with them when they disturbed a snake; running with them when Uncle Stuart put the houseboat into top gear, silently declaring that the race was on; and wishing they'd been quieter when they frightened a raft of ducks.

* * * * *

After a week of adventure-laden days, Eve decided her favourite part had been listening to Grampa's stories about her Mum growing up, their fishing adventures, how she loved to read and how like her Eve was. With Grampa's promise of a surprise to anyone who joined him at 5.30 the following morning, Eve had set her alarm. She'd never been one for early starts, but this bubbly, secretive, fun side of Grampa had her intrigued.

She was surprised how bright she felt when her alarm shattered the stillness of the night; at how quickly her body roused, ignoring the aches lingering after the week's unusual activities; at how cold the floor felt under her feet. She was not surprised that she was the only one stirring, especially with the vague memory of Amanda's phone light twinkling well into the night.

Shrugging into jeans and a hoodie, Eve tried not to disturb her roomies, secretly hoping to have Grampa and his surprise all to herself. She tingled with anticipation, or perhaps it was the brisk dawn breeze hovering over the river as she stepped silently onto the dew-soaked deck that sent shivers through her.

Grampa was alone, leaning against the railing, and Eve drew alongside him. He motioned for her to remain quiet. She heard him whisper 'Good morning,' and followed his nod as he gazed eastward.

She was so glad they were alone.

If the noisy cousins had turned up, the palpable awe would have gone unnoticed.

She could hardly take in the vibrancy of the colours: pink, red, orange, mauve, yellow; every shade of each, the palette changing every moment.

She could hardly breathe, and didn't want to even blink for fear of missing a single nuance of the shimmering glow and the impact it had on the fluid colours of the sunrise.

The sensory feast was totally captivating: the sight of the day's golden prelude; the sound of the river gently lapping against the houseboat and the birds' songs welcoming the day; the sweet smell of the fresh air untainted by city smog. She was so glad to be alive, more alive than she had ever been.

She felt Grampa's arm around her as he gently drew her into a sideways hug. She heard his deep whisper, 'Quite a show, hey.'

Her voice wouldn't work. She stood, cherishing Grampa's embrace, full of wonder at the strange transformation that was working its way through her from deep within. Sharing this extraordinary moment with Grampa suddenly made her feel unique, special, and, best of all, loved.

Somehow it didn't matter anymore that Dad didn't care, was never there. Didn't even send a birthday present. Because she'd shared this sunrise with Grampa.

The cousins chose that instant to burst into the day, and the mood was broken. Eve may have lost the moment, but the memory of that morning would stay with her for a lifetime. She clung to it through the commotion of a big family breakfast, sharing a secret glance with Grampa over the bacon platter. It was still there when

Uncle Stuart beat her soundly at chess, and cards, and Scrabble – she no longer needed to win to feel special.

Envying Amanda and her 'smart' phone seemed crazy now. Her sister might as well have stayed home for all the notice she'd taken of her surroundings. Amanda had missed so much. She'd missed the sunrise.

That evening as Eve squeezed into the smidgen of space they'd left her on the plush, pillow-soft couch, she was elbowed and shoved by cousins trying to race each other to the huge bowl of hot honeyed popcorn that perfectly completed their family movie night.

Eve lassoed a cousin when it was over, ready to piggyback him off to bed, delighted when Grampa harnessed the other and declared a race. She screamed in terror as he collapsed a minute later, dropping the cousin, clutching his chest, gasping for breath.

Uncle Stuart took charge, making Grampa comfortable, comforting Granny, shushing the squealing-but-unharmed cousin. He used Amanda's phone to call Triple Zero and steered them to the nearest dock as fast as he could. Eve helped Granny pack a few things while they waited what seemed like forever for the ambulance.

As Eve returned to Grampa's side, tears of relief fell as she saw his face relax, his breathing become calmer. His eyes were on her with the same sparkle she'd seen this morning. She smiled when he winked in her direction. She knew he loved her, even as he suffered. Eve felt that same inner sensation she'd experienced this morning, sharing the sunrise with Grampa.

She felt peace.

She wanted him to be safe, and healthy, so she could get to know him better. As the paramedics loaded Grampa onto the ambulance, Eve joined the rest of the family in voicing her best wishes. Granny squeezed in next to him, refusing to let go of his hand.

* * * * *

Eve unlocked the front door, dumped her backpack on the floor and turned to help Granny with her load. It didn't matter that the holiday ended early, not with Grampa making a rapid recovery.

As she worked her way through all the settling-back-into-home jobs, she felt the same serenity she had since Grampa's heart turn. She'd had her own kind of heart turn, a turn that kept the sunrise-sensation lingering with her always. She might not have parents who cared enough to be there for birthdays and holidays, but she had Granny and Grampa. They loved her enough to be there every day, for the ordinary days, and for the extra-ordinary sunrise days.

And that was enough.

With age comes... stubborn pride

This is often thought of as a negative trait – the 'stubborn old man' label is rarely considered a compliment.
But, in actual fact, the stubborn pride of an older person is very often a survival skill. It's what makes them keep going.
It's why they get up in the morning despite the pain in their joints, the boredom of the coming day, the loneliness.

And the longer they use their independence and stubbornness to keep themselves pushing forward, the longer they'll be able to. If they give up and let the carer tie their shoe laces, after a while, they won't be able to reach them anymore. If they send the carer shopping because they don't feel up to an outing this week, they'll eventually be house-bound.

That's why the carer's job is to come alongside and help.

To do things with, rather than for.

To encourage the older person to do as much for themselves as they possibly can, rather than swoop in and do everything for them.
That might be quicker and easier, to get the job done, but quick and easy isn't always best.
Better to stand aside and let the older person slowly but surely dress themselves, helping when they ask, than taking over.

Then they'll still be able to tomorrow.

Dear Frederick

Things hadn't really gone according to plan. Not that I ever planned to get old. I certainly never planned to be taken from my home and locked away in a 'residential aged care facility.' That's what they're calling them these days. We used to call them 'Old Folk's Homes'. Now I'm supposed to call it home, but most days I call it jail!

The downward spiral that ended here started three years ago when our daughter, Laurie, came to stay for a week of holidays. She seemed to think we were struggling a bit, and that it was especially hard on her mum. Looking after me was stressful, apparently. Laurie went home again, but rang nearly every night with an agenda for the following day to help Helen and I ride the merry-go-round of meetings, interviews and appointments she'd organised.

Before we knew what was going on, a plethora of lovely young women was parading through the house, doing whatever they could to support us. They helped Helen with the housework and took her shopping. She didn't seem any less stressed to start with. Probably because she'd been doing everything her special way for sixty-three years and getting used to other people in her house was hard. I tried to encourage her to enjoy the break. It was all still getting done, even though they didn't do things her way.

Best of all, we were still together in our own dear place.

When I started needing a rest first thing in the morning after getting myself through the shower and getting dressed, they started helping me with all that too. And when Helen admitted to Laurie that her blood pressure was high despite the doc upping her medication, they sent Steve to take me for outings. To give Helen a break!

It worked both ways, as far as I could see. I got to go out. And I got some male companionship, which had been in short supply since Bruce, my old tennis buddy, and Ken, my best fishing mate, had abandoned me for greener pastures in the Great Beyond.

There's nothing quite as nice as wandering the aisles of the hardware store with someone who understands the thrill of checking out hand tools, power tools, soil improvers and, of course, seeds. Steve got it. He was a bit of a handyman, and, I hate to admit it, knew more about gardening than I'd managed to grasp in all my eighty-seven years.

We ventured out twice a week. When we weren't prowling the hardware aisles, we'd drive along the coast, revisiting my old fishing haunts. And Steve, God bless him, listened animatedly to my endless fishing stories. And my numerous work stories. And my National Service stories. And my hilarious bachelor adventure stories. And my precious family stories.

How I enjoyed those outings. As much as I loved being home with Helen, getting out and about with Steve became the highlights of my week. And I reckon I was easier to live with because of him. I know I smiled more, and didn't mind so much when Helen insisted on reading bits of her gossip magazines out to me. I knew I'd get to talk man-stuff when I went out with Steve.

We settled into the new 'normal' pretty well, until I had a few falls. I couldn't tell you what happened. My jolly legs just seemed to give out and down I'd go. Sometimes I'd get giddy and topple, and if I wasn't quick enough, which, let's face it, I never was, I'd end up on the floor. Poor Helen wasn't strong enough to help me up, so we'd have to call the ambulance. What a tiresome and embarrassing rigmarole!

Laurie came for another visit, and brought a woman from the residential aged care facility with her. She should have been a used-car salesperson. As my brother, Tom, God rest his soul, always used to say about such people, she could 'sell ice to the Eskimos.' She really talked it up, telling us about all the community activities, the thrill of sing-alongs, movie nights, yoga classes every Tuesday morning and, of course, bingo on Thursday afternoons. She really pushed the comradery, the new friendships we'd make, the never-ending program of things to keep our minds and bodies active, engaged and involved.

Whilst I didn't appreciate her style, I couldn't argue with their honest expression of care – they suggested I needed more help than could be provided at home. Helen wept quietly in her chair and I realised that, just like when the drowning accident took our cherished firstborn from us before we'd even sent him off to school, I'd have to be the brave one.

I took in a huge breath and clapped my hands together on the exhale. Laurie and Helen both knew what that meant – I'd made up my mind. And they knew there'd be no discussion or debate.

'How soon can it be arranged?' I asked.

After many more appointments and assessments, we were off to respite. A holiday, Laurie called it, while we waited for a permanent position. And I guess it was rather a novelty. I escorted Helen to the dining room for meals, and we found some old friends to sit with. Jack and Doreen helped us locate Dougie and Jean, some other old friends, and before long we were playing cards and laughing over old times long after everyone else had settled for the night.

Laurie was there to drive us home after that first two-week stay. When she commented how well and happy we both seemed, I had to admit to myself that Helen seemed to be smiling more, and was less likely to snap at me when I asked her to help me with something. She said she'd enjoyed not having to think about meals, or worry if I was going to fall and she wouldn't be able to get me up. I guess men really are thick, like they say, because I'd never really noticed how hard all that had been on her.

Personally, (some might even say selfishly) I was completely content being home again. Back in my own bed, my own chair, and back to my outings with Steve. Then I remembered something my dear old dad, God rest his soul, had told me. He'd taken me aside on my wedding day and shared his secret to a happy marriage with me: 'Son,' he'd said, in the solemn voice he rarely used, 'What's best for the wife always ends up being best for the husband.' I'd repeated it to my sons on their wedding days, and I repeated it to myself again now.

I couldn't ignore the peaceful countenance respite had brought back to Helen's still beautiful face after too long an absence. It lingered for a few days after we got home, but was slowly eroded by worry lines. For her sake, I began to look forward to another respite visit. Somewhere along the way, I even accepted going in permanently.

Until they told me I'd be going in alone!

Some rot about Helen not being poorly enough to qualify for permanent status.

Things went downhill fast from there, for so many reasons. My attitude stunk, I'll admit it, but it was more than just me that was the problem. The timing was terrible. A room became available on, of all days, March 15th and so, instead of celebrating sixty-four years of marriage with fish and chips at our favourite picnic spot on the coast, I was barking orders about how I wanted my sons and son-in-law to arrange the furniture in my new room. I hated myself for being so grizzly. I hated this stinking situation even more.

I hadn't even had the chance to say goodbye to Steve.

I tried really hard to remember why it had to be this way, especially when I drew Helen into my arms to say 'Happy Anniversary' one last time, and, in the next breath, 'Goodnight', even though it was hours before bedtime. I smiled and pushed her out the door, waving as she walked down the wide corridor, clinging to our eldest boy, Richard. Then I slammed my new door, closed my new curtains, curled up on my new bed, and, forgetting I was meant to be brave, cried like a baby.

A week later, Covid hit.

They cancelled Movie Night. Sing-alongs were banned. Yoga classes, the only thing I had no intention of ever attending, happened with the regulatory social distancing...whatever that meant. Thursdays held no appeal without bingo.

My world, which had shrunk overnight when I'd moved here, shrunk more as the month went on, until all I had to look forward to was seeing Helen every other day, and meeting our old friends in the dining room. But that tiny joy just wasn't the same without Helen.

Then Covid came real close, and my world became a prison, although I reckon inmates of those 'residential facilities' get time out in the yard. We weren't even allowed to wander up and down the corridors for exercise. I ate increasingly unappealing meals in my room. Worse still, Helen couldn't visit.

We talked on the phone, but neither of us was doing anything, so our conversation was strained after only a few minutes. I assured her I was doing okay. She did the same for me. I began to worry she was lying as much as I was, to make me feel better.

Television was the only entertainment left, and Covid filled the screen, no matter what time I tuned in. The staff were overworked and worried all the time. They tried to encourage me, to spread cheer instead of gloom, but when I asked straight out about our friends, I knew from Sophie's eyes the news was bad. Doreen had succumbed, God rest her soul. Jack was in the hospital, clinging to life by a thread. And Dougie was on oxygen in his room.

To hell with being brave. When she left and closed the door I thumped the back of it. I threw a cushion across the room. Then I slumped into my overstuffed new chair and…stared at the wall.

Even crying seemed too hard.

Later that day, just before she went off shift, a timid Sophie gingerly opened my door, waving a letter. She seemed to think it was something worth getting excited about, but she didn't have Helen with her, so I wasn't sharing her enthusiasm. She put it on my side table and left.

It was the middle of the night, when sleep evaded me yet again, that I remembered the letter and sought it out. Well, at least it wasn't a window envelope. My name and address were hand written, so it likely wasn't some charity begging funds. With a spark of curiosity, I ripped it open and began to read:

Dear Frederick,

I was so sorry to hear that the transition to your new home has been a stormy one. Life everywhere has changed, for all of us. One thing they haven't banned, so far at least, is fishing. I went last weekend with my boys. You should have seen...

I wasn't sure whether to laugh at the antics of Steve and his boys, or cry because it proved I was wrong... I hadn't been forgotten after all. I knew it was from Steve the moment he asked about my 'top-secret' red hooks... my advice was still valued. It ended with a vital offer of hope...

I'll write again soon,
Your friend,
Steve

Right then, in the wee small hours, I rummaged around for a writing pad and countered his fishy tale with two of my own. I threw in another story from my dear old Dad's outback adventures, and one about the first car I ever owned, and was licking the envelope before I realised I'd not mentioned Covid, or life in the jail once.

In the coming weeks, I didn't know what brought greater contentment – reading letters from Steve, who somehow managed to sound as though he'd read every rambling word of my letters, or writing back. Sometimes I had a letter half-written before Steve wrote again. I blathered on about National Service, various jobs I'd had, and highlights from numerous family road trips. For over a month, I anticipated mail call as much as I looked forward to hearing from Helen.

Finally, the penny dropped. If I was having so much fun, why not share the joy. I turned over a fresh page and began...

Dear Dougie,

and when I'd finished sharing memories about the fish, and the girls, that got away, I started another page with...

Dear Jack,

That one had to be more serious. He'd lost his wife, after all. I had no wisdom to offer, no great words of comfort, other than to promise him a game of cards when this was over.

Before long, letters were flying back and forth between us old geezers.

And with each letter sent, and every one received, my world grew bigger again. Steve was planting a garden, and asked for advice on fertilizing. There was life beyond me and my room. I'd made some alterations to the cubby-house plans Steve had sent for my perusal. There was news other than Covid – Dougie was off oxygen and feeling good, at last.

This darn virus had bowled its best at us – the illness, the isolation, and the anxiety. But it hadn't had the final say. By banding together by mail, we'd risen above everything it'd thrown. Together apart, we'd prevailed.

'Getting old is like climbing a mountain;
you get a little out of breath,
but the view is much better!'

Ingrid Bergman

On the Clifftop

South Australia had experienced its warmest June for fifteen years, its driest for ten. The farmers were complaining, but not us. We'd made the most of the exceptional weather, reacquainting our dear friend Maureen with the delights of our region. She'd been part of our family for forever, it seemed, and was one special lady.

She was visiting from overseas, having been away for twelve years. She wanted to hug a gum tree, see some kangaroos, walk on the beach, and eat a pie-floater. The weather had been perfect for it all.

Until the end. Late in the month, a cold front brushed the south coast. It didn't matter quite so much the day we did the road trip to Cape Jervis, although the fog made it hard to catch a glimpse of Kangaroo Island. We shunned the outdoor tables at the beachfront café, watching from inside as the grey sea churned and the black clouds rolled in from the west, then dashing to the car before the deluge began.

It bucketed down all night, waking me several times. This was not the gentle patter of rain that makes sleep return easily. This was the noisy pounding that makes you grateful for a solid roof overhead. And I was.

I was equally grateful to get a phone call in the morning, inviting me to join in once again. We'd taken turns to host

Maureen. Mine had been last week, in the sunshine, giving Dad a chance to recover from the flu. Now it was Dad's turn, and I appreciated them sharing it with me, especially since Maureen would be going home next week.

Weather permitting, Dad and his wife planned a cliff-top walk after lunch. They'd ring me if it was happening. It was raining as we spoke, so I doubted it would happen. *Weatherzone* predicted strong winds and scattered showers.

Staying in and chatting over a nice cup of tea sounded good to me, but the phone call I presumed would cancel the walk, instead confirmed it. I was to be at their place at 1:30 and we'd be back by 3 for that cup of tea. Hopeful patches of blue sky broke through the clouds as I headed for my car, the freezing cold forcing me back inside to dig a coat and scarf out of the far corner of the wardrobe.

We left my car at King's Beach, the endpoint of the walk, with the hand-brake firmly on against the slope. Dad drove us all in his car to where we'd start. And drove. And drove. From dirt road, to dirt track, to long, winding driveway, dodging the scattered debris from last night's storm: puddle-filled pot-holes, deep ruts turned to rivulets, small branches tossed down by the wind. And sheep. We were well and truly in the middle of nowhere, the back of beyond, way past the black stump.

We left the car on a friend's property, and walked to the Heysen Trail. Any doubts about the weather were blown away by the view. The wide blue sky, trimmed with white clouds, thin and billowy. The huge expanse of ocean, deep blue, edged with white foam against the cliffs. Sunny. Still.

Majestic.

We headed off, spirits high, with no idea what we were in for. We walked, and chatted, and laughed through thin scrub, admiring native plants along the way. Every time we saw a little trail marker, Dad would say, 'It's good to know we're on the right track.' The track was level and wide, making puddle-dodging easy – either stepping over or around them, even when it meant making a new path through the trees.

The level track soon narrowed to barely wide enough for two feet together, forcing us into single file, and silence. It was cold. That chat over a cup of tea was looking better all the time, except for the incredible view.

The narrow track, barely even a bunny trail, soon turned downward, and with the gentle slope, things got slippery. The scrub was thicker, and came right up to the trail on both sides, leaving us no way to avoid the puddly, muddy, boggy mess. We were forced to navigate loose stones, puddles and overhanging branches. No time now to admire the view. We had to concentrate on each step, striving for a sure footing every time.

Treacherous.

About an hour into the walk, the sky darkened, the wind picked up, and the trail turned steeply uphill. Climbing on slippery ground was difficult and tiring. When we reached the summit, we stopped for a break and Dad undid the backpack.

'Any Fruchocs in there?' I asked, thinking that would be a fitting South Australian memory for Maureen. And a happy snack for me.

'Just water,' he said after catching his breath. They'd always been the ones to model healthy eating habits.

Not long after our break, the rain began. This was no scattered shower. This was rain. We kept walking. There was nothing else to do. Wet jeans slapped against my weary legs with every laboured step, the added weight making walking harder.

Miserable.

I was stuck on a cliff edge in the pouring rain, with my father in his eighties still recovering from the flu, and two women not much younger. If one of them slipped and broke a hip, it would be me who'd have to run in search of unseen civilisation, or to find somewhere with phone reception so as to alert the helicopter rescue team. Me who, just two weeks ago had been ambulanced to hospital with a rapid and highly erratic heartbeat. More alarming still, no one even knew we were here.

My senses were filled with a strong feeling of something bigger than me drawing near. Was that the Almighty whispering into my heart, '*I know exactly where you are*'?

We pressed on. It was just as far to go on as it would be to go back. Each step became a slow and calculated process to avoid slipping. The rain had stopped, but the wind worked with our dampness to chill us to the bone. We stopped frequently to rest, and plan our strategy as the slopes got steeper. With each rise I hoped to see the car, only to have the trail head back down into another gully, no end in sight.

'Any almonds in there?' I asked Dad after we'd been walking two hours. Even a healthy snack would be welcome.

'Just water,' he said again.

Maureen found some Sesame Snaps in the pocket of her coat. I should have known God would provide. He not only knew where I was, He knew just what I needed.

Energized by our snack, Maureen and I tightrope-walked along opposite edges of the track, which had been sunken by so many feet before us. We held hands across the muddy divide for balance. Dad fell further and further behind, perhaps not as recovered from his flu as he'd thought. We rested often, because we needed to, and to give him time to catch up. And we prayed. Out loud. For Dad. For all of us. For sure footing, and strength to make it to the car.

A mob of kangaroos watched us from a grassy clearing up a hill. Probably thought we were crazy, working our way through mud that would sooner slide out from under us than hold us up, with no foothold, no trees to clutch at for support, and the sheer cliff-face less than a metre away. They were probably right, but we had no other choice. To keep going was the only way out. Any pleasure in the trip was gone. Only perseverance remained. The end was all that mattered now.

Down another perilous hill and up the other side, we saw it. Better than the cliffs, the seascape or the scrub, it was my little green Mazda in the King's Beach car park, just visible as dusk settled over the coast. It was still a frighteningly long way off, but we at last had something to aim for.

With our soggy spirits slightly bolstered by the vision of our goal, we hobbled on, wretched, weary, wet and freezing. But we were not alone. We had each other, and God was with us.

How do I know?

Because we made it. Exhausted, but whole. Nothing sprained or broken. Even my erratic heart had behaved.

Those final steps to the car in near darkness were the hardest, but oh, how heavenly to sink into its shelter. I drove us back to

Dad's car. We'd all sleep well tonight, we said, laughing about it now.

'Was it worth it?' some have asked.

'Without a doubt,' I say.

It gave me so much. Priceless photos of the view. Precious memories of an adventure shared with people I love, people who might not be around to share too many more adventures. Powerful lessons about the walk each one of us takes through life.

And it gave me this story to tell, of walking with God on the clifftop.

'There is a fountain of youth:
It is your mind, your talents, the creativity you bring
to your life and the lives of people you love.
When you learn to tap this source,
you will truly have defeated age.'

Sophia Loren

Hope in Flames

Later I'll realise how eerie the timing is.

I shouldn't even have my phone on me. Thank God I remembered to turn it to vibrate, since that's precisely what it starts doing as the crematorium staff lower my father into the furnace.

Although I'm trying hard to focus on the here and now, I spare a moment to be grateful my phone is in my left pocket and my distraught mother is on my right, leaning heavily against me, barely able to hold herself up. I'd hate the incessant buzz of the phone to interrupt her mourning.

Not that focussing on what is happening is all that easy. It's rather ghastly, in fact, to imagine my dad being engulfed by flames. It seems the opposite of everything Dad was, every memory I have of him. When I was a boy, my dad was always striving, always doing, always achieving the best. Whatever the lads in the schoolyard came up with, my dad did it better than any of theirs. He had a better farm and a finer horse than their dads. He could ride faster, fence straighter and shear closer.

He was my hero.

I didn't tell the boys he also gave the warmest hugs, told the most exciting bedtime stories, and loved my mum so much he cried when she nearly died having my little sister. But those are the things I'd remembered as I grew up and found a wife of my own.

And as I faced the challenges of parenthood, I tried to do it Dad's way, because Dad was the best.

Dad was a fighter. He'd fought bravely in the war and had the medals to prove it. He'd saved the farm from the flood of '59 through sheer will-power, sandbagging the bulging creek single-handed while his brother took the stock to higher ground. And years later, along with everybody else in town that day, I heard him fight the bank manager out of foreclosing on the loan.

It doesn't seem right imagining the big, strong man that was my dad lying helplessly in a casket being consumed by flames, without a fight.

It wasn't just us family that thought the world of Dad. He was an elder in the church, a volunteer for the local CFS, a general all-around good neighbour. If anyone needed help, they knew Dad would be there, offering muscle-power, equipment, wisdom, sympathy or anything else that was needed, even the shirt off his back. He was everybody's mate.

And yet it's just Mum and me standing alone in this sterile house of death. Again, I'm grateful. This time, that Dad doesn't know it. He'd always imagined a big funeral, with his four children and fifteen grandchildren and twenty-three great-grandchildren. All of us together, celebrating his life, his heritage, his legacy around the barbie following the burial.

Now it's Dad's coffin the flames are licking, rather than the sausages Uncle Tom would have burnt for certain.

And Mum and I are a very long way from the family farm, and the community that loved Dad.

They'd been on the trip of a lifetime, celebrating sixty years of marriage and getting in early for Mum's eightieth next month. It was a big thing for them at their age, and the first overseas holiday they'd taken. For so many years Dad couldn't, or wouldn't, leave the farm. Then he discovered how much fun it was exploring his rugged, sunburnt country.

But Mum wanted more than another caravan trip to honour their sixty years together, and Dad couldn't deny her dream. They boarded the cruise ship hand-in-hand, easily as starry-eyed as the honeymooners they shared the gangplank with.

Then it all went pear-shaped.

They'd toured the Cotswolds, strolling cobblestoned lanes, marvelling at the lush green countryside, then dining on fish and chips at a local pub. When they returned to their hotel, Dad went to bed while Mum stayed up to write on the postcards she'd bought.

She knew something was wrong as soon as she went to bed – the snoring that had been a part of every night for the past sixty years was silent.

And Dad was cold in his bed.

He would have loved going that way – quick and painless, except for the anguish it caused Mum.

Chaos erupted. Who knows how Mum managed navigating her way through ambulance rides, hospital waiting rooms, and endless red-tape. Alone.

Someone eventually rang me.

It'd been a hot, dry summer back home, and we were running out of feed, carting water and scouring the sky for signs of much-needed rain. That's where I was when my phone rang and a stranger told me Dad was dead.

Through the fog of grief and shock and worry, one thought remained constant – it was a lousy time for me to leave the farm. I was certain Sharon, my sister, would be more of a comfort to Mum, but as Dad's power of attorney, it had to be me.

Ten days later, here we are. And my phone is buzzing again.

Again, with Mum sobbing softly beside me, I can only ignore it.

It's late before I finally get Mum settled and remember to check my phone.

Five missed calls from home!

Too tired to calculate the time difference, or the cost of international calls, I simply hit the recall button. When no one answers, I sink into a sleep riddled with nightmarish flames.

Sorting red-tape and keeping it together for Mum takes every bit of my concentration for days, especially when Mum starts having dizzy turns and ends up in hospital. I slump into a stiff waiting-room seat and stare blankly at the sub-titled TV screen, until the vision grabs my full attention.

Australia is alight with bushfires.

And I never did get through to home.

My imagination races to the worst scenario – complete destruction, with flames licking at my family as they had my father only days before. I stand and pace and fumble with my phone until I finally hear the heavenly sound of my wife, my precious Caroline, alive. Sinking into the grey, hard seat, I listen.

The house is gone. The stock as well. And dear old Jack from down the road. Our sons, having lost their valiant fight against the flames on our place, are off fighting for someone else's.

I hear the heartache in my sweet Carol's voice. My arms long to reach out and comfort her.

'Mum's not too good, love... I'll get there as soon as I can... I'm so sorry,' I wonder how much she's heard through her weeping.

Then I hear her take a huge breath. I imagine her straightening her back, squaring her shoulders.

'We'll be fine,' she says. 'Don't worry.'

There's the woman of strength I know and love so much.

Mum's doctor approaches.

'Gotta go, Love. Talk to you soon. Love you.'

My torn heart turns from one tragedy to another, closer but somehow less traumatic now. At least I can do something here.

Or not.

Mum's had a stroke. It'll be several weeks before she can travel.

Weeks full of frustration. Weeks that start out with me scouring the television for news of home, but soon find me avoiding it. It hurts too much to see reports of continuing devastation and not be there to help. I've never felt more powerless.

Like Dad lying there letting the flames swallow him.

I've seen bushfires before. Fought them alongside friends and neighbours, all of us refusing to give up on our land, our livelihood, our mates. Now all I can do is sit halfway across the world, helping Mum with her therapy and choosing an urn for Dad's ashes. If it wasn't so pitiful, I guess it might be funny.

Eventually, I choose to be grateful for little things. Small steps forward in Mum's recovery. Travel insurance covering much of our costs. Reports of soaking rain extinguishing the fires at last.

* * * * *

Nearly two months later, we arrive back in Australia, Mum in a wheelchair, Dad in his urn in her lap, and me ready to kiss the ground in deep appreciation of being home, where I belong.

My son David's there to meet us. He holds the welcome hug a little longer than he might have, hinting for just a moment at the rough time he's had.

It's a long drive home, and with his grandma safely snoring in the back seat, still hugging the urn in her lap, David opens up. First about the family – all alive, thank God, though Geoff, my other son, burnt his arm pretty bad. Then about our place – the house completely gutted, the stock incinerated, the outbuildings razed. And next about the rest – neighbours mostly in the same position we are, the local school lost, the church still standing somehow, but with smoke and water damage.

As we drive through what looks like a post-apocalyptic movie scene, I see the damage for myself. So extensive. So complete. Having lived it all before, I know how hard it must have been to be here, but I also know there must be more, something that's broken David's spirit.

We're nearly home before he tells me gruffly, 'I couldn't save him, Dad.'

I reach over and squeeze his shoulder, 'Who is it, Son?'

'Mick,' he manages.

There's nothing I can say. He's lost his best mate. We journey on in silence.

It's surreal to finally be here. Home. There's nothing like it, though it's nothing like I left it. I see they've got a pretty fair set-up happening, with a borrowed caravan, some tents. It's clear they've already started preparing the place for rebuilding.

Then I'm holding my precious Caroline, feeling her welcome strength as I trust she's feeling mine. And never wanting to let her go again.

It's days before Mum's ready to say goodbye to Dad again, but it's what Dad would have wanted, to be buried on his land. He'd picked his spot years before, and, miraculously, the tree on the hill overlooking everywhere survived the fire somehow.

So that's where we gather for the big funeral he'd always imagined, better late than never. His four children, fifteen grandchildren and twenty-three great-grandchildren, and half the district. All of us together, commemorating his life, his heritage, his legacy.

A breeze stirs up the stench of fire and the memory of seeing Dad engulfed by flames. I see again that dark, hidden place where my hero was reduced to ash, just like the farm around me. Looking across the great bunch of people who loved Dad, I wish he could've seen them, survivors every one of them, looking to the future with determination.

Just like he always had.

I thought I was facing a bleak future without him, but I was wrong. He'll live on as a legacy of strength in each one of them, and, yeah, in me too.

Walking back from Dad's tree, arm in arm with Caroline, tiny tufts of green catch my eye – new life rising from the ashen landscape. It hits me that mere ashes can't rob me of a future here, just as they can't rob this family of our hero. My future is safe within the strength of these people, these brave, strong people who refuse to be beaten by hardship, each one as much a hero to me as Dad was. As the rain brought fresh growth to the ground, greener than we'd seen for years, that thought brings hope to my worry-worn soul.

Uncle Tom's on barbie duty. It's time to brush the charred bits off a sausage and celebrate being alive.

With age comes... laughter

Sometimes, older people are funny.
They might do funny things, or say funny things.
They may even look funny.

The really important thing is to laugh **with** them,
rather than **at** them.

Laughing at them often comes easier,
when they give an odd answer
because they didn't hear the question right,
or talk to themselves because they are so used to being alone.

The harder, but more worthwhile thing to do
is to laugh with them. Harder because it takes time to draw
alongside them, get to know them,
and appreciate their unique sense of humour.
They may use words they laugh at that don't mean much to you
unless you take the time to ask, and listen for the answer.
They more than likely have lots of funny stories to tell,
if you take the time to sit with them for a while.
And listen through all the stories, some sad, some funny.

Don't think that because they don't laugh all the time,
because they seem to have lots to complain about,
that they don't enjoy a good laugh –
all the better for sharing with someone
who's taken the time to understand what's so funny.

Nan's Final Wish

Melody struggled with the legalities of death. How could they be reading Nan's will when they hadn't even buried her yet? And where were her sisters?

She sat in the stuffy, leather-scented outer office of Demurrer, Malfeasance and Tort, Attorneys at Law.

'One of the associates should be with you shortly,' claimed the crisp, well-dressed receptionist, barely glancing up from her typing. Melody wanted to ask whether her tight hairdo resulted in headaches, but didn't think the woman would see the humour.

Finally, an austere man in his fifties approached, shook Melody's hand and introduced himself as Archibald Appellant, not one of the names on the door. If this guy couldn't make it, what on earth did it take? He certainly looked the part – his grey hair and black suit perfectly matched the dark woodwork in the outer office.

The heavy, depressing décor extended to Archie's office. If only Melody could let loose with her unique interior design flair, she'd brighten this place up in a whirl – add some colour, some plants, some modern artwork. This oppressive style did nothing to alleviate the gloom of grieving clients, or those facing legal difficulties. And surely no one but the legally desperate would venture into this distinguished domain.

Archie pulled her out of her redecorating reverie with a polite cough.

'Miss Broad, your grandmother wanted you to have this.' He held out a large manila envelope.

'We surely can't start without my sisters, Mister…ah…'

'Appellant,' he filled in for her. 'This matter does not concern your sisters, Miss Broad. This is a personal matter between you and the deceased.'

Flustered, Melody took the envelope. 'I'm sorry. I don't understand. Am I the only one mentioned in the will? That doesn't seem right.'

'This is not the last will and testament of Mrs Dorothy Broad. It is merely a personal correspondence from my client to you.'

Despite her persistent confusion, Melody tried to instil confidence into her 'Oh! I see.'

'I'll give you some privacy while you explore the contents. My next appointment is in ten minutes.' Archie rose and left the room. Too bad if she needed longer than that to 'explore.'

Nan's neat curly-loop script addressing the envelope to her brought tears to Melody's eyes. Nan had been more mother to her than grandmother. Twenty years ago, when their parents were killed in a boating tragedy, Nan and Pop took eight-year-old Melody and her two older sisters in and raised them well.

Melody marvelled that so much of her character could be directly attributed to Nan – her passion for reading, her love of long walks in the country, even her finesse for interior design. She well remembered her surprise at being allowed to choose paint colours, not only for her own bedroom, but for the whole house.

Nan was good at that – discovering the girls' talents and encouraging them to pursue their interests. It was Nan who taught Ginger to cook, then celebrated her success when she won prizes at local shows, eventually hosting her own cooking show on TV. It was Nan who passed on all her gardening knowledge to Rosemary, who now ran a successful chain of landscape gardening stores. Each of them owed their achievements to Nan. They all owed her so much.

And now she was gone.

A cough brought Melody's journey down memory lane to an abrupt end. Did the man have a lung condition, or was he conveniently able to produce that annoying sound on demand?

'I'm sorry, Miss Broad, but, as indicated earlier, I require my office for another appointment.'

'But…I'm not done…I haven't even opened…'

'My secretary will be in touch to arrange a time for the reading of the will. May I convey the condolences of all of us here at Demurrer, Malfeasance and Tort, Attorneys at Law.'

By the time he'd finished this cold, impersonal speech, Archie was holding the door open for her, looking impatient for her removal.

Melody quickly collected herself and her things and stepped into the outer office. She just as quickly dismissed the idea of sitting here to read whatever was in the envelope. Instead, she made her way out of the building and across the road to a park. It seemed far more fitting to spend her last moments with Nan on a bench under a sprawling gum tree than in a stuffy legal office.

When she opened the envelope, two items spilled onto her lap – a ticket to a Symphony Orchestra concert for the following evening and a letter.

Curiosity overcame Melody's desire to linger over Nan's beautiful handwriting, the scented floral stationery, or the date at the top of the page – just days before she'd died. She could sit and dwell on the memories, or she could find out what on earth this was all about.

Guilt seeped through her memory-softened heart as she read how disappointed Nan had been that Melody hadn't planned on accompanying her to the concert. It had been a bit of a thing with them. Every couple of months they'd see a show or attend a concert together. Nan claimed she wanted to broaden Melody's cultural horizons. When it became apparent that what she really wanted was to find Melody a cultured husband, Melody had backed off, finding excuses not to go with Nan.

Nan took credit for finding husbands for both Ginger and Rosemary. She thought she was ever so clever to match chef Ginger with Tom Waldorf, giving her the surname of the salad she loved to prepare. Nan was equally delighted to team Rosemary with Glenn Oakes, a well-respected arborist who was employed at the Botanical Gardens, but flew all over the world to consult on issues of tree health. Whether Nan had anything to do with her sisters finding the men of their dreams or not, both couples were happy and successful, and that's all that mattered to Melody.

She wondered which of Melody's talents or interests Nan would choose to match her man to, and how going to concerts would hasten the process. But she was determined to find her own man.

So she'd bowed out of the concert, claiming another commitment.

It seemed, though, that even from the grave, Nan was determined that she go. 'It's clear that I won't be able to make it,' she wrote. 'I likely won't even be here to wave you off, or wait up to hear all about it when you get home. So go in my place, Dearest Melody. Close your eyes in the midst of some musical masterpiece and think of me. I'll be humming along as I dance with the angels. Don't you be sad for a minute. I've lived a good life. My only regret is not seeing you get married.'

Sadness overwhelmed her, and Melody had to look away.

She sat there, on a bench in a park and cried. She cried for all she had lost. She cried for all Nan had been to her – her mother, her best friend. Most of all she cried because she wasn't sure she'd expressed to Nan how much she loved her. Had she died not knowing?

After a long time, Melody wiped her eyes, blew her nose and stood. She would go to the concert. She would honour Nan's final wish.

* * * * *

Nan had stressed the virtue of punctuality to Melody for twenty years.

Unsuccessfully.

Parking was a nightmare, the ridiculously high heels that Melody had worn to honour Nan's dress code for such events made it impossible to run, and, to seal her tardiness, one of them snapped clear off as she attempted to hurry up the stairs.

Bells were sounding and doors were just closing when Melody limped to the entrance allocated on her ticket. It looked like she might be waiting in the foyer until Intermission, until the usher spotted her gold-class ticket and reopened the door. She even offered to help her find her seat, guiding her to the front row with a smile.

Before Melody had caught her breath after her frenzied dash for the door, the orchestra filed onto the stage. While they settled, she took the opportunity to bend down, slip her unfortunate shoes off, and stow her bag under her seat. When the audience burst into a round of applause, Melody sat up and looked forward.

Straight into the deepest pair of blue eyes she had ever beheld.

They were set in the handsomest face she'd ever seen. The rugged jawline underscored full red lips, curved upwards in a teasing smile. The features were perfectly proportioned. The colouring was straight out of her what-to-look-for-in-the-perfect-man list. And the cheeky twinkle in those stunning eyes suggested that he may have been as surprised to see her bobbing up from her crouch as she'd been to see him so suddenly appearing.

And so breathtakingly close.

Before she remembered to breathe, the lights dimmed. Just as she lost connection with those dulcet optical pools, the broad shoulders somewhere beneath her focus gave a slight shrug and the face, the shoulders, the man turned away. He had a job to do, after all. One that necessitated having his back to the audience for the rest of the evening.

But what a back it was! Gee, could he fill a suit. The few concerts she'd managed to attend with Nan had mostly involved long, sleepy sorts of pieces. Melody remembered one in particular in which every piece had the word *adagio* in the title. They heard Adagios in both G and D minor, *Adagio for Strings* and Adagios by

Rachmaninoff, Mahler and Mozart. When she'd tactfully commented how peaceful the evening had been, Nan informed her that adagio was a musical term meaning slow, to be performed with the greatest amount of grace. The conductor that night had what could only be described as an incredibly average back.

Even now, as the exuberant and unashamedly joyful overture to Mozart's wonderful *The Marriage of Figaro* mesmerised the audience, Melody was utterly spellbound by the stretch and flexibility of the fabric of the conductor's suit. Not to mention how the seams somehow endured the full range of shoulder movement and energy this man, this muscular musical maestro gave to this piece. Again, Melody found herself forgetting to breathe.

And completely convinced that even this amount of rhythmic exertion could never result in such exquisite tone, such magnificence of form, such abundant fullness beneath his expensive, tailor-made suit.

He obviously went to the gym.

Lots.

Next on the program was Vivaldi's *Four Seasons*. The orchestra might have only been performing *Spring*, but this conductor, this batonic virtuoso fitted a year's worth of weather and emotion and movement into his performance. He used every gorgeous part of his lithe body to draw the best from the musicians, and when they finished, there was a prolonged silence, a rapt stillness before the transfixed listeners erupted in appreciative applause.

The lights went up, signalling the approach of Intermission. The conductor turned, bowed with such style and grace Melody thought he must surely be of royal descent, and made as if to leave the stage. Then hesitated. Scanned the front row. Locked eyes with Melody. And grinned.

She stood. Moved forward, drawn like metal to a magnet. He leaned forward to say, 'Are you enjoying the performance?'

She could listen to that for a lifetime. Perhaps that should have been her answer. However, 1) she was too awestruck to put any words together with any sort of actual meaning, and 2) that inner dialogue was referring to his voice, which conjured images of the smoothest, creamiest hot chocolate in front of a huge fireplace. Or standing at Niagara feeling the rumble of the falls through every cell in her body. Or getting caught outside in a thunderstorm, the intensity of nature's display arousing every sense.

The subtle clearing of that enticing throat brought her from her musing with a jolt. What was the question again? Was it her turn to talk?

'Enchanting,' she murmured. His polite nod and his smile, which would have sent her back to Niagara if she hadn't looked away quickly, convinced her that whatever she'd said must have been appropriate.

After several more minutes of staring into each other eyes, someone on stage sidled up to the conductor, tapped him on his powerful broad shoulder, and whispered something in his ear.

'Aahh. Sorry, I must go. They can't leave the stage until I do.'

Whoops. Her ogling had stopped these wonderful musicians getting their caffeine and sugar fixes, their bathroom breaks, their stand and stretch.

She reluctantly broke the tie that invisibly bound them to one another and began to move away. He held up a finger, the very finger that could create mesmerising music. She experienced the power of that finger, drawing her back to him.

'Don't forget your shoes,' he whispered, making full use of that grin again. And with yet another wink, he was gone.

And Melody stood there, eyes fixed on the exact point at which he exited the stage. Then someone politely touched her elbow, and informed her that part of the gold-class experience was a champagne supper in the adjacent ballroom. She quickly collected her shoes, tucked them under her arm, and hurried after the usher.

Intermission became somewhat of an orchestral meet and greet for gold-class audience members. It was all Melody could manage not to constantly scour the room for her conductor, until she overheard someone else enquiring after his whereabouts and being told he wouldn't be in attendance.

'He needs to rest up for the second half.'

And Melody, though consumed with disappointment, completely understood. To perform with such passion, such energy, such overwhelming devotion and enthusiasm, would be exhausting.

The second half proved to be just as stimulating as the first. Nicholas performed with equal zeal. Melody had looked up his name in her program and nearly swooned, again, the way Nicholas Maestoso rolled so well over her palate as she murmured it over and over again. If her memory of musical terms from all those piano lessons Nan had insisted upon was right, Maestoso meant majestic.

Like his suit, his name fitted him perfectly.

Rather than being enthralled by Nicholas's back, Melody raised her sights to the back of his head, to the exquisite mahogany mane dancing over his white collar in glossy waves.

She imagined what it would be like to run her fingers through it, like swirling them through a pool of chocolate. Salted caramel chocolate. Sometimes Nicholas (oh, how she loved knowing his name) thrust his head with such vigour some of the luscious locks fell away from the rest and Melody had to clasp her hands tightly in her lap to resist the urge to adjust them.

She was relieved when, as one, the entire company turned their pages to perform Boccherini's pretty *Minuet,* prompting thoughts of Nan. She would have so loved this piece. She would have loved Nicholas. The mischievous matchmaker in her would have loved that Melody was already well on the way to loving Nicholas.

As the delicate harmonies settled deep into her soul, Melody closed her eyes and imagined Nan, free from illness and the crippling effects of age, dancing with angels. Despite Nan's written instructions to the contrary, tears flowed down Melody's cheeks as she realised that, although Nan was likely content, they'd never again share a special moment together.

The music changed yet again, and Melody was thrust out of her grief by a paroxysm of fervour which shot through Nicholas to the orchestra and on to the stunned audience as Tchaikovsky's *1812 Overture* energised every particle in the room. The torrent of dynamics stole their collective breaths. The frenzy of movement from Nicholas was enough to make the best of them dizzy. They moved with him, rocking back and forth, swaying, and finally, rising as one in an ovation of applause.

When he turned and bowed, Melody froze. Applause continued to swell around her, but she stood motionless, utterly hypnotised by the deep blue eyes which found hers in the crowd, held hers even as he bowed, until he turned again to salute the musicians.

And then he was gone.

Melody felt lost. Cold. Numb. Empty.

As if her heart had ceased its job and left her clinging to life.

Until once again she felt an usher touch her elbow. Dear Nan wasn't yet finished with her matchmaking shenanigans. Melody's gold-class ticket apparently entitled her to go backstage and meet the conductor. Alone.

Now she was flustered. What would she say? Was her hair still in place? Oooh, she needed the bathroom. She needed to breathe. She needed...a moment.

She missed Nan.

Nan would have known just what to say. She would have smiled at Melody with a gentle, 'You look perfect, Dear.' Nicholas and Melody would have naturally been comfortable and at ease together under the influence of Nan's aura of tranquillity. And then, giving some completely sociably acceptable excuse, dear Nan would have discreetly left them to their mutual attraction.

Abandoning her broken shoes, Melody retreated to the bathroom barefoot, primped her hair then proceeded to give herself a Nan-worthy pep-talk. She could do this. Nan had taught her to embrace every challenge as an opportunity. To conquer every fear with courage borne of a strong foundation of self-esteem. To believe in herself. She could almost hear Nan saying, 'He's the lucky one, Dear, getting to meet with you backstage.'

Melody was convinced that, to Nan's way of thinking, tonight had less to do with a single evening of musical entertainment, and more to do with a lifelong love like she'd had with Pop. After all, she'd given Ginger and Tom a jumpstart down the road to love, and ensured Rosemary travelled the same way with Glenn. From

Melody's perspective, her gold-class ticket was Nan's way of setting her and Nicholas up to make beautiful music together for a lifetime.

She'd resisted all of Nan's previous attempts at playing Cupid, but this was different. This was Nan's final wish. Besides, there was that spark, that irresistibility, that nine-on-the-Richter-scale force of attraction between them that warranted investigation.

She inhaled deeply, checked her makeup one more time and exited the bathroom.

She didn't want to keep her hunky conductor waiting.

'The best tunes are played on the oldest fiddles!'

Ralph Waldo Emerson

That's why we do Social Support
– A Poem

When I saw Alf on Wednesday morning,
There were no dishes in the sink.
When I asked him what he'd had for tea,
He had to really stop and think.
'Getting old's a bugger,' he moaned, then, 'I'm just waiting round
to die.'

I mentioned then about his friends,
The ones who'd moved away.
'They're coming back to see you, Alf.
We'll have lunch with them Friday.'
He smiled at that, the old spark back, then, 'Will you make a cup of
tea?'

On Friday he was up and dressed, saying
'It'll be nice to be with friends.'
'How 'bout you take your birthday cards.'
The fuss for being a hundred extends.
'Not everyone has one from the Queen,' I tried. Then, 'What a
great idea.'

When I returned to pick him up
He held a bag of cards.
He wore a clean shirt and a smile
And strode ahead by yards.
We had to detour to collect his meds, then, 'There they are, I see them.'

There were extras there to see the friends
Hugs and handshakes did abound
Alf smiled and laughed and ate up well
And passed his cards around.
'You're the best you've ever been, old friend.' Then, 'All the carers help.'

We sadly tore ourselves away,
'Let's do this all again.
Next time you come, give us a shout,
And I'll be here with Alf.'
'Nice to see them.' 'Yes indeed,' then, 'I look forward to when they come again.'

'You can't help getting older,
but you don't have to get old.'

George Burns

The Legend of Paddy O'Malley

Paddy had needed to get out. He couldn't stand the closed-in feel of the stark apartment a moment longer. It was far too cold to walk the streets. Or sit in the park.

'How are you this fine winter's day?' chirped the overly cheery librarian as he entered the old building adjacent to the council chambers. She gave her name, expecting his in return. He merely nodded in reply, thinking libraries were meant to be quiet, serious places.

'Anything I can help you with today?' she flustered.

'Just browsing.' Paddy made his way towards the big window, away from the desk, and the likelihood of further forced conversation. He'd be warm here, and could still look out over his favourite place, the local park by the river. The closest he got to wide open spaces these days.

He sat on the well-worn couch and felt something odd. Reaching beneath him, he pulled out a book, abandoned lazily by its previous reader. He moved to put it on the table next to him, but a glance at its title caused him to pause:

The Pioneer Flame

'Might be interesting,' he mumbled to himself, opening the cover.

An hour later, the jolly librarian bustled over, asking if he'd like a coffee. Nice thought, he supposed, but she was interrupting his reading.

'Thanks,' he barely looked up to follow her point as she indicated the machine in the corner.

A stretch might be good for his legs. She'd broken his concentration now anyway.

Rather than have to talk, he grabbed his drink and settled back in his spot. He wasn't feigning his fascination with the book. Before the interruption, he'd been reading about Charles Throsby, a doctor on a convict ship in 1802. Must have been a good one too, since none of his convicts died, at a time when death was inevitable on the long sea voyage.

Throsby was an important man in the fledgling colony of New South Wales, as doctor, magistrate, explorer and grazier. He was one of the first to open up new land beyond the Blue Mountains for colonial settlement.

In his droving days, Paddy had ridden through some rough country on the plains, and could just imagine the trek over those mighty Blue Mountains, travelling through Banjo Paterson's *'stringybarks and saplings, on the rough and broken ground... where mountain ash and kurrajong grew wide.'* It would have been far rougher than anything he'd ever faced.

In Paddy's eyes, Throsby was a true pioneer, not just exploring, but remaining to overcome the hardships of terrain and weather to settle the harsh Australian bush. He'd built roads, owned land and cattle, and kept exploring to provide more rich land for others. He'd even been appointed to the New South Wales Legislative Council.

Paddy sipped his coffee, staring out over the park towards the Murrumbidgee River, thinking about courageous men willing to make a go of life in a new place. A harsh place. A place that seemed determined to stop them.

Such thoughts came mighty close to being self-condemning, so he returned to his reading. He turned to a section on the life of Captain Charles Sturt, a pioneer of the Murrumbidgee, and his expedition to find its mouth. What a brave pioneer that man was, but Paddy was intrigued to discover much more about him than he'd heard before. It seemed Sturt was a praying man. He took a Bible with him on his treks into the unknown and slept with it under his pillow. He even prayed about his journeys, committing his safety to the Almighty. Seemed like it worked, too.

At one stage, Sturt and his party were short of supplies and had to make it 900 miles upstream in the same time it had taken to travel downstream. Paddy knew enough about the Murrumbidgee to know that was impossible, especially against the strong current with low rations.

But Sturt did it.

He did it faster.

And he thanked his God when he made it back alive.

Paddy couldn't stop reading. Next was a chapter about Edward Flood, who owned over 76,000 acres of pastoral land in this area in 1848, a station called the Narrandera Run. Paddy had just read about this successful, wealthy politician and his very humble beginning, when his tummy began to growl. Looking at the clock, he realised it was protesting the time.

He needed lunch.

He'd grab something quick and come back. Oh, sure, he could borrow the book. But he'd have to speak to that woman. And register. Forms. Details. Too hard.

He'd come back after a bite to eat.

'What will it be today, sir?' the young waitress bubbled. Everyone in this town was so friendly. Perhaps it was her genuine smile, or maybe 'the pioneer flame' was getting to him, but he smiled back and ordered a sandwich and a coffee. Those people he'd spent the morning with hadn't approached others with reserve. That was no way to succeed when you are breaking in a new land. They were quick to make friends because they relied on each other for survival in this vast, lonely place.

'There you go, sir. Are you just passing through town?' She placed his order in front of him. Paddy took a deep breath. He could do this. Of course he could. He'd never been shy around the campfire. In fact, he was usually the first to start a conversation. So many stories to tell back then.

'No. I've recently moved into town. A flat just off Moreton Road.' There. That wasn't so hard.

'That's a lovely area. Have you got family in town?'

'No. No family.' Not here anyway. The folk back out west were like family to him. Well, north-west actually. As close to family as he'd ever have. Mates as good as brothers, for sure. They'd seen each other through the best and the worst. Worked hard alongside each other. Played hard too. Such memories.

She must have noticed the faraway look in his eyes. 'Hope you aren't lonely then, sir?' She looked around. 'The place is pretty quiet. I could sit for a while if you wanted company while you eat. If you liked, that is?'

He remembered *The Pioneer Flame* and gave her a nod. Before he knew it, he'd told her about his fifty years working the outback station. About the campfires and the droughts. About his mates that were like brothers. He'd even told her about the dodgy ticker that eventually forced him into town to be closer to medical care. How he'd picked this town because of the river. How his mate's daughter lived here and kept an eye on him.

She'd sat transfixed, egging him on with nods and questions.

As if suddenly realising the extent of his ramblings, he shifted in his seat, packed up his dishes and started to stand.

'I wish you had more time. I love hearing your stories. I've learnt more today than I ever did in history lessons.'

He knew she meant it as a compliment, but it made Paddy feel old. Maybe old-but-interesting wasn't a bad thing to be.

'Thanks for your company,' he smiled at her and meant it. 'I'll be back another day. That was a good sandwich.' Truth was he'd been so busy tripping down memory lane he couldn't even remember eating a bite. It was the company he'd enjoyed. Having someone to talk to.

When the chatty librarian welcomed him back, he thrust out his hand to shake hers. 'Paddy O'Malley's the name.' They'd spent the morning together, after all, so he guessed she deserved to know his name.

He'd done enough talking for the day, though. More than the average week's worth recently, just over lunch. He retreated to his spot by the window and retrieved *The Pioneer Flame* from beneath the cushion.

Before he knew it, she was standing next to him, telling him the library was about to close for the day. Again, time had passed without him noticing.

'I'll be back tomorrow to finish up,' he said, hurrying away before she mentioned signing up.

Walking home through the chilly evening, he found himself humming an old bushman's song. He thought of what he'd learned about Peter Dodds McCormick this afternoon. He'd been working as a stonemason at a church. His cheerful singing while he worked caught the ear of the minister, who invited him to join the choir. He'd gone on to lead huge choirs, including 20,000 voices at a Sunday school centenary celebration.

And he'd composed *Advance Australia Fair*. From the privacy of *'joyful strains'* on the job, came the very public salute to our *'golden soil and wealth'* and *'Nature's gifts of beauty rich and rare.'* Paddy knew he'd only ever sing in the shower. But he could hum. Maybe if he hummed more, he'd seem less gruff to others. It might even help him feel less gruff.

His little flat didn't seem as bleak when he pushed the door open as it had when he'd left it that morning. While he heated a can of soup, he remembered reading about Elizabeth Macarthur. Now there was a busy woman. Seven children. Controversial husband who wasn't always there when she needed him. She educated the kids, grew fruit and vegies to feed them, managed several huge properties, bred sheep for better wool production, and supervised convict labour, all while remaining a model of good character to all who knew her.

Quite a woman.

And certainly a pioneer.

He couldn't remember all of them now, but as he gave thanks for his humble tucker, he remembered feeling a special kinship with Father Patrick Hartigan. They shared a name, after all. And Hartigan was described as handsome, kindly and shy. Paddy had to stop the comparison there, since Hartigan was a priest, educator, author and poet. Paddy certainly wasn't.

Father Patrick would have been a great encouragement to his outback pastoral flock, with his strong faith, his understanding of the bush, and his respect for the mateship that binds bush folk together. His poems celebrated their lives, and *The Pioneer Flame* celebrated his.

It celebrated the lives of many pioneers. Men and women, armed only with stubborn character and sheer determination, who stood firm against the hardships, dug in deep and built the foundations on which Australia grew. Some barely survived. Others made a success of it for themselves and a future for those that came after them.

But it wasn't only the next generation that benefitted. Paddy was making a fresh start in a new place. There was a lot he could learn from those pioneers. Why, he'd already gained some of their wisdom and through it had made a new friend at the coffee shop. She'd even thought he had something to offer with all his stories. Maybe she was right. He had, after all, been a pioneer of sorts, in the outback all those years ago.

An idea landed on him with such force he was glad to be sitting down. His mate's daughter taught at the local school. If the young waitress at lunch time had enjoyed his stories, maybe he could tell them to Debbie's class. Even better, he could include stories from *The Pioneer Flame*. Then, when those children faced new challenges, they'd have the wisdom of the pioneers to strengthen them.

That's how the pioneer flame could burn on. The kids of today could discover excellent role models from Australia's history to help shape their identities for the future. They could learn about the courage, vision, and sacrifice those pioneers needed to build the great nation of Australia. They could learn about the mateship and perseverance that grew out of hardships they faced together. The past mattered. There were qualities in those pioneers that would help today's young people succeed in their future. And ensure the future success of this nation.

The flame was burning in Paddy, with all the force of a raging bushfire. He just had to pass it on.

He'd phone Debbie now.

'Old age is like everything else.
To make a success of it, you've got to start young.'

Theodore Roosevelt

School Bus 908

The sign on the side of the road said, 'CLEARING SALE', but the old place screamed 'fire sale'. It'd seen better days. Gates hanging off their hinges were propped against sagging fences. The yard around the house was overgrown with weeds. Rusted gutters hung precariously from tilting verandas.

I'd loved clearing sales as a child, mostly for the Saturday away from farm chores they gave me. And the chance to explore with mates. They were the social highlight of my small world. Everyone turned out for a clearing sale. Finding a bargain was a bonus.

Turning into the pot-holed driveway, I knew this one was different. This one meant another farming family was going under. Drought, economic climate and politics had got the better of some poor hardworking bloke and his equally hardworking wife and kids, forcing them off land that had likely been in the family for generations.

I'd read it in the papers, seen it on the news, but as I stood in the junk-filled yard of that run-down farm just one valley over from where I'd grown up, it really hit me. Aussies on the land were doing it tough, and I'd lost touch. This was more than a distant national crisis. This was close to home.

I walked along crooked rows of tools and farm equipment. An over-zealous agent worked hard at selling it.

'The bigger stuff's out behind the sheds,' he repeated as each group filed past.

I rounded the corner and saw a dilapidated old friend, a grey Fergie tractor. Cowering behind it in shame lay an old school bus, like the rotted carcass of a beached whale. Dry weeds grew wild and tall around flat tyres. Its rust-eaten paint had been bright yellow in its heyday. Its windows were broken. Headlights too. Moving closer I could just make out its sun-bleached number, 908 – my old school bus. Rural decay suddenly got personal.

Instantly, I was four years old again, bouncing along in the cab of our old Dodge ute, peering longingly at my much older brothers and sister laughing together in the back. They seemed so excited, so connected. We always got to the end of our road just as the dusty yellow bus snorted around the bend and groaned to a stop. The clever folding door opened wide and my family pushed and shoved their way up the steps. Then they were gone, swallowed by the heaving monster.

I couldn't wait to be five. Then I'd be old enough to go with them on their adventure, instead of going home with Mum to entertain myself while she worked. All day I waited for her to make her cup of tea. I gulped down the milk she gave me, knowing that as soon as we were done, we'd drive back down the road and wait for the bus.

Finally, it arrived, and spewed my siblings onto the road. They laughed and waved frantically to their yellow four-wheeled friend, then clambered into the tray of the ute. They were so happy after a day with that bus. If only I was big enough to join them.

Standing as a grown man, staring into the blind eyes of School Bus 908, I laughed at the naiveté of that four-year-old me. And at how quickly things had changed.

I turned five just before Christmas, and as my family celebrated a new year, I looked forward to new beginnings – riding the bus with the big kids. At last, the day came. Cherie, my big sister, helped hoist my brand-new backpack – weighed down as it was with a lunch box stuffed with sandwiches and fruit, and my new red drink bottle – up into the tray of the ute. Everything was labelled, right down to my jocks.

I was one of them at last, a big kid, jostling along in the back, clutching the edge in fear of bouncing right over it. They were laughing and excited as always, and I wanted to join in. I just wasn't sure what they were excited about.

We heard it coming long before it got to our stop, whining and rattling its way along the country track. When it arrived, I was nearly knocked flying in the crush as the others grabbed their packs and rushed for the bus. They barely paused long enough to turn and throw a wave Mum's way.

I froze, torn between wanting to hurry forward with them, and wanting to cling to Mum, at least long enough to hug her goodbye. What lay within the clanking yellow shell? I only knew the others loved it. Was that enough? All I knew just then was that I loved my mum and staying behind with her suddenly seemed like the best thing.

My bottom lip wobbled. My knees shook. My arm trembled at the weight of the backpack, which fell to the ground in a puff of dust. My tummy flip-flopped and I worried it might expel my Weetbix breakfast. Mum didn't stop smiling and waving. Cherie came back down the steps, put one hand on my shoulder and picked up my pack. Gently, she guided me up the steps.

'Don't worry, kiddo. You'll have fun.'

I tried to answer, but my throat felt tight. No words could get out. She pushed me into a seat at the front, thrust my pack into my lap, then sat behind me, waving her friend Helen forward to join her. I heard my brothers laughing from way down the back.

The driver, Mr Hudson, pulled a lever and the fancy folding door stretched across the mouth of the bus with a screech. I looked beyond it and saw the ute already heading up our road. If the weight of my backpack wasn't pressing me into my seat, I might've dashed after it, after Mum.

But she was gone.

Perhaps now the fun would begin. Except it didn't. The bendy road, with its steep hills and treacherous curves, seemed endless. The noise of gears grinding interrupted daydreams of what I'd be doing if I was home with Mum.

No matter how many times we stopped, and how many kids climbed up those steps, no one joined me in the front seat. They merely smirked and hurried past, already talking to kids further back.

We bounced along forever, my teeth chattering with every bump, my body swaying with each bend in the narrow country road. Finally, we stopped. The creaking door unfolded. A stampede from behind forced me to stay in my seat, kids pushing and shoving and dragging their backpacks. I was last off, hoping this thing called school would be less bumpy than the journey here.

I already hated that bus, but it was my only way home, and I was pleased to see it that afternoon. Until I burnt my legs on the hot seat. And discovered the windows didn't open. It was like sitting in an oven. But an oven that would take me home to Mum.

Cherie whacked me on the shoulder when we got to our stop. Somehow, despite the noise of the bus and its occupants, and the roughness of the ride, I'd nodded off. Some of the other kids in my class had gone home not long after lunch, but us bus kids had to stay all day. I'd never been so pleased to see the ute, and Mum. Instead of clambering into the back with the others, I sat in next to her.

'So, what did you get up to today?' she smiled. I wanted to say I'd missed her. I wanted to say I hated that rattly old bus. I wanted to climb into her lap and stay there forever. But I knew that would never do.

'We did some colouring. And pasting. They let me bring a book home to read.' I tried to pick out the high points.

It wasn't long before the journey on School Bus 908 became a tolerable means to an end, and, as with most new beginnings, I stopped wishing I could go back to staying home with Mum.

'Brings back memories, doesn't she, Robert?' I wasn't that fearful five-year-old anymore. I was at a clearing sale, and someone knew my name. I had no idea who stood next to me, gazing at the broken-down bus.

'Sorry, do I know you?' I replied, putting my hand out to shake his. We were in the country, after all, and country folks were friendly.

'Pete Willsmore. We went to school together, on this very bus. Haven't seen you in ages.'

'I haven't been back in years,' I released his hand and walked away, down the side of the bus, not quite ready to explain.

How could I have not recognised Pete, my old best mate from school? We'd met on this very bus. He sat across the aisle from me one morning, finishing his reading homework, like me. All of a sudden, he was throwing up. What a stink! My tummy started feeling funny, all twittery and churny and I wished those bus windows opened. Fresh air would've felt good.

I turned away and breathed deeply, feeling better. Until Pete threw up again, splashing vomit over my shoes. Yuk. That's when I joined in the puking. And Pete and I became mates.

I was drawn back to the present by a tug on my sleeve.

'Hey, Mister, want some lemonade? Or maybe a slice of cake. We've got banana or chocolate.'

Not what I'd expected. No sign of Pete.

'Sounds perfect,' I smiled and the girl, about the same age as my granddaughter, Dianna, led me back around to the house yard. Her sister manned a folding table and handed me chilled lemonade in a paper cup.

'That'll be a dollar, Mister. For two you get a slice of cake to go with it.'

'I'll have banana, thanks.'

The slice was huge, the cake a little dry, but I admired the girls' enterprise. My grandkids wouldn't be safe doing anything like this in the city. And they were always busy with friends, sport, music lessons, and mostly, it seemed, technology.

'This the old Hudson place?' I asked the woman who brought more ice from an esky in the boot of her car. She was obviously the girls' mother. They had her chestnut hair.

'Did you know my father?' she answered with a sad smile.

'Spent a good many hours on that old bus with him,' I said, waving in the direction of the vehicular graveyard out the back. 'What happened to him?'

He'd struggled with the farm for years, she told me, supplementing his income with bus-driving through one drought after another. Things got more and more run down. When her father lost his bus licence, a cousin tried to help, but couldn't work with the cranky old man. He insisted everything be done his way, the old-fashioned way.

'My father died a few months back,' she finished, looking around at his life's legacy. 'I hate to sell it all, but Mum's in the nursing home, and none of the family want to take it on.'

'I'm sorry for your loss.' I'd finished my cake. There seemed nothing left to say, so I wandered around some more, drawn back to the decrepit bus like a blowy to fly paper.

By the time I was fourteen, all my siblings had left school. Pete had been shipped off to finish high school in the city. It felt like I was starting over again.

I said a dreary 'Hi' to Mr Hudson and walked up the aisle. There was one seat left, about halfway back. Next to a girl. I held myself stiff through all the bends in the road so as not to sway into her. I glanced sideways. Pretty. Long blonde hair swept back in a shiny ponytail. Cute little nose turned up at the end.

I couldn't help but notice she wore her school skirt much shorter than Cherie ever had. Her slender legs were tanned. I was relieved to get to school so I could stop fighting the temptation to reach out and touch her skin. It looked so smooth.

She was in my class. All the boys gawked at her, preening and strutting about like roosters with a new chicken in the henhouse. But I'd seen her first.

I raced to sit next to her on the bus going home that first day. And the next. And every day after that. Marion and I studied together in our free lessons, though never on the bus. No way would I risk humiliating myself by throwing up in front of her.

On the bus, we'd talk. And laugh. I never knew a girl could be a best friend. She congratulated me on topping the class in Maths. I held her hand as she cried after a snake bite killed her dog. When I needed a date for the school dance, I naturally asked Marion.

And when it finally came time to leave the farm and move to the city for Uni, I couldn't bear the thought of going without my best friend. My girlfriend. My Marion. We were married over the summer break and started a whole new life. A life so busy, and full, there was no looking back.

Until now. Clive, my older brother had worked our farm alongside Dad, then with his own sons when Dad passed away. I'd returned only for a minimum of necessary family occasions – three weddings and two funerals, each time staying for the least possible time, never really taking an interest in the farm, or my brother's lifestyle.

And yet, standing in the shade of a massive gum, the wide blue sky peeping through grey-green leaves, the fresh air filling my lungs, staring at that broken-down bus, I'd discovered something magical about coming back. About looking back. Despite my full city life, my successful career in sales and my complete lack of interest in farming, my past was bursting with rich memories. Some sad, most not.

Perhaps leaving everything behind had been a mistake. This ramshackle place, with its derelict bus, had given me something I wanted to embrace all over again, and, most importantly, something I knew was important to share with my family, especially my grandchildren – the wide blue skies, the fresh farm smells. And, best of all, my school bus stories.

I'd made this trip reluctantly. There were some big decisions to make about the legacy of land my father had tamed, and worked, and left as our shared inheritance. This detour had brought back the past I'd turned my back on, in full living colour, albeit a little rusty round the edges. My family had missed out on growing up in the country, and I'd need to bring them soon if I wanted them to get even a small taste of it the way it was.

Before time and drought, economic climate and government policies changed it all again. Before the crumbling heap of rust before me lost its battle with the elements. And before my grandchildren grew up and started over somewhere else again.

But first, I needed to track Pete down, and see what he'd been up to since our days growing up together on School Bus 908.

'Age is simply the number of years the world
has been enjoying you!'

Unknown

It Takes a Village

'You got it right, Dot, dying when you did.' I notice the cheap plastic flowers, well and truly faded now, leaning against the dark granite tombstone. My wife of sixty-four years likely deserves better, but I'm still so angry with her, even after twelve years, that I refuse to do anything about it.

'You left me here and now I've lived too long. Everything hurts. And nobody cares. You should count your lucky stars you went when you did, before arthritis gnarled your fingers, your knees, your hips …and made every movement agony. Before you turned into a walking pill bottle, with a different one added every time you see the doc, which is way too often, to counter the side effects of the last one they gave you. Before they took away your driver's licence, just because of your age.'

It's that last one that really makes me mad. There was nothing wrong with my driving. Damned cop saw my birthdate on my driver's licence and decided then and there that people who've lived ninety-eight years shouldn't be behind the wheel. I did everything he asked me to do, and did it safely to boot. But, no, he'd made up his mind.

'So there's no more lunches with the gang at the café, no more popping down to the bank or the shops when I feel like it. I've got to phone the blasted taxi! That's what I get for living too long. There ought to be a law against it.'

My neighbours have offered to take me places, but I'm not interested in asking those gossipers for help. I'd have to explain where I was going and why, and it's none of their business. They'd want plenty of notice too, I guess, and I'm not one to plan too far ahead. Besides, I intend to hang on to my independence, and my privacy, for as long as I can. They don't need to know how many times a week I go out for lunch.

A car horn interrupts my bitter musings.

'That's the taxi back to take me home, Dot. Don't know when I'll get back to see you. Make the most of wherever you've found yourself. Gotta be better than here.'

The taxi driver knows me better than to bother with idle chit-chat, and I've only been using him for a week. Smart man. Guess he learned his lesson after I responded with a series of grunts the first time he bothered trying to start a conversation about the weather. Weather doesn't matter to me anymore, since I won't be fishing with Tom, gardening with Dot, or bowling with the boys at the club that made me a life member thirty-five years ago. It might as well rain every day for all it matters to me.

As we pull into my driveway, I glance around, then look away.

'Looks like you could do with a hand around here.' I'd forgotten the taxi driver was still here. He probably thinks I'm not up to dealing with the weeds pushing up between cracks in the concrete, and infiltrating Dot's prize rose beds. Or the cobwebs smothering the windows and hanging from the eaves. Or the leaf litter overflowing the gutter. As if it's any of his business.

'Just because that dang cop took my licence off me doesn't mean I can't aim a weed-wand,' I retaliate, standing a little taller, 'or wave a broom. Or even climb a ladder for that matter.'

It's not that I couldn't if I wanted to. It's more that I simply can't be bothered. A few weeds never hurt anybody anyway. What does it matter?

'See you next time, then, Jack. Take care of yourself.'

'Well, if I don't, no one else will, that's for sure,' I think aloud, my words drowned by the departing taxi.

Shuffling inside, I kick a pile of old newspapers out of the way. I should really throw them out, but I can always get to that another day. It's time for a cup of tea right now.

There're no clean cups in the cupboard. Digging through the contents of my sink, I find one and rinse it under the tap. That'll do.

While the kettle boils, I realise I'm hungry. There's plenty of food in the house – frozen pies, tins of soup, snags. I even bought some of those lamingtons with jam through the middle, like Dot used to make for Sundays, only not as nice. None of it appeals at the moment, so I rummage through the sink and find a bowl to rinse, then reach for the breakfast cereal. Looks like I forgot to roll down the top last time I used them. Oh well.

A rush of foul-smelling cold air hits me when I open the fridge for milk. Must have left something too long. I'll have to clean it out.

I'll get to it later, after my cuppa.

Settling my bowl and cup in a bit of clear space at the table, I notice my staggering collection of pill bottles, and wonder if I've taken any today. Better grab a few to keep Emma happy. My granddaughter means well, but all she seems to do these days is fuss and nag. Am I eating right? Have I taken my pills? Have I showered today? What about changing my clothes?

As if I'm her child instead of her grandfather.

I mean, I love the girl dearly, and I feel like an ungrateful old grump, but if all she's going to do is get at me, I'd just as soon she not make the two-hour trek to visit every fortnight. I'm on edge the whole time she's here, expecting her at any moment to bring up the dreaded 'N' word. And I will not let her put me away in a nursing home.

I push the unfinished bowl of dry cereal away. Such depressing thoughts have chased away what little appetite I had. My knees crack and crunch as I stand and walk to the lounge room, easing my old bones into my favourite chair. I choose to look beyond the neglected front yard, over the rooftops of my nosy neighbours to the sea. Looks like a good day for fishing...

It's a relief to wake up several hours later. Even though I was only nodding in the chair, I'd dreamt. A terrible procession had marched before my sleeping eyes. My old mates from Kokoda, some who didn't make it home, others who'd passed since, led the procession, followed by our daughter Susan, who'd been taken from us far too soon by breast cancer. It's never a good thing when a parent has to bury their only child. Next came Dot and my brother and three sisters, all younger than me but gone just the same. Bringing up the rear were my best fishing buddy, Tom; my old tennis partner, Bruce; and all the boys I beat at bowls until they deserted me fifteen years ago.

Seeing them all again might have made for a pleasant dream. Instead, their jeers, their laughter, their haughty waves, their chants of, 'We got out while the going was good,' and 'You've lived too long, Jack' turned it into a nightmare and left me feeling more alone than ever.

November 8ᵗʰ 2019
'Hello Dot,' I say, bending over carefully to place her favourite vase full of roses on her gravestone. 'Your roses are looking beautiful this year, so I brought you some.'

The hand I've come to rely on lately is there for balance as I rise. 'I've brought Leah with me, or rather she brought me. We're on our way to lunch at the café, with Max and Mavis, and Irene. Now, don't go getting jealous, will you Dot,' I give Leah a wink, 'just because I've got a harem of lovely ladies looking after me now. There's blokes too, you know.'

I argued with Emma till I was blue in the face – I didn't want the help she kept trying to organise. In fact, I didn't want any help at all. I was managing well enough on my own and just wanted to be left alone.

I'm sure I don't know where that girl got her stubbornness from, but she persisted. Brought a steady stream of people through the house. They asked question after question, offering this, that and the other, and blow me down if Emma's 'Yes' to every offer didn't seem to carry more weight with them than my oft-repeated 'No!'

Especially when they got Doc Evans involved, with his, 'What'd be the harm in giving it a try, Jack?'

Then I fell and gashed my leg and it was, 'Accept the home help, or it's a nursing home for you, Grandad,' from Emma, and the same from the Doc, except he calls me Jack.

'They say wisdom comes with age, Dot. Well, I reckon it's taken me ninety-nine years to get smart, apart from the little burst of brilliance when I asked you to be my wife, of course. So I gave in and signed their twenty thousand forms, and everything changed.'

Now my place is like a train station, bustling with people coming and going, and full of rails, in the bathroom and loo, and at the back steps, so I feel safe all the time now. I make sure I'm up, showered and dressed by nine every morning, so I'm ready when someone comes to make the bed, see to breakfast and dish out the morning pills. They somehow have time to chat as well, so I try to hear the news on the radio first thing. Then I'm up with the latest to make conversation. The cuppa they leave me with always tastes better than the ones I make myself.

Then someone else comes by later, and we go out to lunch, or shopping, or for a drive. My favourite trip takes us along the coast to all my old fishing haunts, especially when Martin takes me – he falls for the tallest of tall fishing stories every time. Ha! But he talks with me like an old mate, and knows about cars and farming and the garden.

Wednesday's the only day we stay home. Debbie comes to clean. She moves like the wind, changing the sheets, getting the washing on, then zipping around with the vacuum cleaner until it's time to hang it out. She's so fast we often have time to 'attack the clutter' as she calls it. No more paper piles to dodge on the way in, and we've unearthed some real treasures.

'That reminds me, Dot. We found the jewellery box your parents gave you on our wedding day, with your grandmother's cameo brooch tucked into the little drawer. Hadn't seen it for years. Emma was delighted when I gave it to her.'

Someone else comes in later each day too. They dish out my evening tablets, and help me decide what to have for tea. On Wednesdays, they bring in the washing and the smell of sunshine and washing powder on my towels and shirts reminds me of when my Dot insisted on hanging washing outside even after we saved up for a drier.

Even the Doc seems to think my old ticker is the best it's been for twenty years. He puts it down to taking the right pills at the right time. And that only happens because someone comes every morning and every evening to get them for me.

Every day is special now, but Thursdays are probably my favourite. That's the day Martin and I go for lunch at The Lakes Café. It's where we met Max and Mavis, one day when the place was packed and they asked if they could share our table. We've shared a table and a bowl of chips every Thursday since then, and I really look forward to chatting with the boys. Max is an old farmer just like me. He even spent some time in the outback, working in a mine just like me, only twenty years later than I did.

'Emma's started planning the party already, Dot. Gee, I wish you could be there. Emma assures me there'll be a letter from the Queen.'

For ages, I never dreamed I'd live to be a hundred. Then, for a whole lot of years, the thought of doing so became my worst nightmare. Now, I can't wait. All the family are coming, and Max and Mavis, and their friend Irene, who keeps Mavis company at lunch while Martin and Max and I talk about men's stuff.

'I've even applied to the powers-that-be for them to allow all my wonderful carers to come, even though they're not supposed to see me out of hours. Surely turning a hundred warrants some sort of special exemption.' I wink at Leah, whose standing patiently at a distance, not wanting to intrude on my time with Dot.

'You know, Dot, how, I used to complain about how often your parents visited when Susan was young, and about how long they stayed. You'd say, "Well, Jack, you know it takes a village to raise a child. They're an important part of our village." Well, I'm starting to think it takes a village to make it to a hundred. And I want my entire village to celebrate with me. I'll tell you all about it next time I visit.'

With age comes... legacy

There are a lot of humble older people out there, who don't think
they have anything to offer any more. They've no doubt lived their
long lives putting one foot in front of the other,
getting by the best they could.
And now they have more time to reflect,
they may well wonder what it was all about.
They may even long to leave a legacy.

It may be money, property, faith, business, life values,
or any number of things.

They want future generations to know they were here.
They want to know their lives meant something, that they,
somehow, made a difference.
They want to leave an impression.

The thing with legacy is that it goes both ways – like money in a
will, it needs to be given and received.
One of the best ways to bless an older person
is to let them impress you.
Listen to their stories and advice, give weight to their wisdom.
Accept with gratitude their gifts of sometimes strange,
but always cherished artefacts from their lives.
Let them have an impact, no matter how small, on your life.

Drawing alongside an older person might even change you
for the better, and give you a legacy to leave.

A Promise for Ada

'I promise, Grandma,' she patted my hand like a mother comforts a sick child. 'It's late. You get some rest. I'll be right here when you wake up.'

I wanted to believe dear Annabelle, my great-granddaughter, who had flown in from Sydney after a stroke put me in this wretched hospital bed. She'd arrived with flowers, chocolates and a bulging bag of new nighties for me. She'd been here ever since, except for bathroom breaks. I knew she was sincere, but I'd given up on promises long ago.

The gnarled fingers of my good hand curled around her slender, youthful one as if to soak up her strength and use it to keep her here should she renege on her promise. Dear Annabelle bent over and kissed my cheek, then settled back in her chair, quietly humming the hymns she knew I loved.

My rest was fitful, a conglomeration of pictures filing across the fuzzy screen of my mind. Were they memories or dreams? Really, they were more like nightmares.

A man's face, contorted beyond recognition or description. A long, evil laugh echoing around me, almost drowning out his cries of, 'I never promised you anything.' I couldn't recognise him because I'd never seen him, yet somehow, I knew he was my father. He hadn't cared enough to hang around beyond conception.

All the unspoken promises that came with having a father were denied me – provision, protection, princesshood. They say you can't miss what you've never had, but I seemed to have a gaping dad-shaped hole inside me that refused to be satisfied with any substitutes.

The next picture in the parade was merely a shadow. A whisper. A woman's face, hollow eyes rimmed in darkness. Thin, reddened hands dragging four-year-old me from one poorhouse to the next, hissing at me to stop crying. 'Things'll be better soon,' Mum had promised, between hacking coughs.

I don't remember much about the last night I had a real mum. She shook me awake and hauled me out into the darkness. Pinned a note to my thin frock. Clasped my face between her trembling hands for the longest time. Gave me one final kiss, laced with the salt of her tears. Then she pushed me into a doorway, squeaking out one last promise between sobs. 'Don't move, sweet Ada. Things will be better now, I promise.' She banged loudly on the door and ran.

I almost believed then that promises do come true. The food wasn't much, but it was regular, at least. And sleeping in the same bed night after night was a novelty I could get used to.

Until the foster home relay started. Time after time, people took me into their homes, promising the nuns they'd love me as their own, only to send me back. Their faces passed by quickly in the nightmarish procession, accompanied by sounds of slapping, shouts and scolding. The memory filled my body with the ache of chopping wood and too many household chores. I could smell the booze again. What was wrong with me? Why couldn't anyone love me?

Finally, someone did. The Praters took me into their home when I was ten and once again promised to look after me. They gave me a room of my own and bought new clothes for me. They sent me to school with nice lunches and didn't make me do housework or dishes every night. I found myself humming on the ride to school and skipping home from the bus stop every afternoon.

But after several years of such wonderfulness, things began to change. I was growing up. The big boys noticed my developing figure about the same time I did, and sent wolf-whistles my way, making my less curvaceous girlfriends jealous. That was the least of my worries.

I awoke one night to find Mr Prater in my bed, one hand across my mouth, the other exploring parts of me I barely knew existed. When I tried to scream, he pressed against me all the harder. I can't remember how long he stayed. Or when he left. Only that I woke up crying. Then... and now, to find my dear sweet Annabelle's hand in mine. Still, I couldn't shake the terror as I drifted back to sleep.

He'd wanted me to call him Daddy after that. But Daddies were supposed to offer protection, provision and princesshood, weren't they? Mr Prater tendered only humiliation, hurt and horror, as the nocturnal visits continued several times a week.

Everything changed after that. Mrs Prater hated me and cried all the time. Mr Prater came home late smelling of beer and cigarettes. I ran away three times and three times well-meaning neighbours delivered me back into Mr Prater's anxious arms. Even when I made it to my best friend's house, her policeman dad refused to believe my accusations, calling me a trouble-maker whilst driving me 'home.'

I made sure my fourth attempt succeeded soon after I turned fifteen, pinching the stash of cash they kept in the bottom kitchen drawer and catching a bus to Sydney. The Air Force was recruiting and I easily passed as eighteen once I'd put my hair up and balanced in a pair of stolen high heels.

It seemed my first independent decision was a good one. I was trained in telegraph operation, given a uniform and a home with other girls, and generally treated with respect. The food was good. I only went once when the girls invited me to join them for a drink after work. That was all it took for the smell of beer and cigarettes to set me to puking in the lady's room, my head spinning with awful memories.

Soon enough, I caught the attention of the men I worked with. But one in particular, Max, made sure none of the others did anything more than tip their hats and smile on the way past. Only he was allowed to linger, and linger he did. The way my Max made me feel was nothing like I'd felt with Mr Prater. With my Max, I felt cherished, treasured, safe.

When Max promised to have and hold me for better or for worse, I forgot all the broken promises and echoed his 'I do.' We had days of happy memory-making, of 'normal married life', of wedded bliss and laughter. Days spent together, having and holding, just like my Max had promised. His gentle love cut through my painful past. I saw a bright future, full of hope.

The nurse came in with breakfast, and seemed surprised to see me smiling. The memories of marital harmony and happiness would have made that smile cheeky but Nurse Simms would never know the reason given the lopsided nature of the grin. I was embarrassed to have my precious Annabelle attempt to feed me.

She insisted, struggling to contain the mess and maintain my dignity as sloppy mush went everywhere.

Opening a half-numb mouth, and swallowing tiny spoonfuls of tasteless stuff was exhausting, and happy memories of my Max pulled me back into a peaceful slumber. My addled mind forgot how quickly peace betrayed me, turning slumber into struggle once again.

Because it wasn't long before my Max was called up for active duty. Long enough to leave me pregnant as he sailed away to war, and alone when our first child was born. Perhaps it was the damage done by Mr Prater's abuse, or punishment for any part I might have played in that dastardly sin, but whatever the reason, it soon became clear that Raymond wasn't normal. He was sweet and simple and loving, but his muscles and his heart lacked strength.

There were doctor's visits and tests, special formula and many sleepless nights of worrying and wondering, alone. Then word came that my Max was coming home, despite the ongoing war. That meant only one thing, which became all too apparent when I saw him. My Max was injured. There were doctor's visits and tests, special diets and many sleepless nights of worrying and wondering, still alone, as my Max lay sleeping restlessly in the next room. He couldn't, or wouldn't, share my bed.

After months of painful therapy, my Max recovered physically. The Air Force gave him work to do, and life returned to a new normal. There was having and holding once again, and two more sons were born. They were strong and healthy, and did all the things young boys do. I learnt to drive to take them to hockey games in winter, tennis in the summer, and to the beach whenever it was warm enough.

Raymond went everywhere with me. Mainly because I wanted him there, watching his brothers, cheering them on. But also because his father, my Max, couldn't bear to look at him, let alone care for him without me.

Gradually, over the years, there became more and so much more that my Max couldn't bear to do. He never spoke about the war. I knew the horror was beyond description. I heard it every night as he relived it in his dreams, thrashing about, screaming, or sobbing in remembered pain.

Yet he refused my comfort, refused to enjoy our sons, refused more and more, to have and hold as promised. Until one day, he left me. Oh, he didn't walk away, or even take the bus – no, my Max hung himself in the basement while I was at the hospital with Raymond, again. The note in his jacket pocket said, 'I'm sorry, Ada. You'll manage better without me, love, I promise.'

It was sadly hard to miss him, since he'd only really been a shadow. A man in body only, an empty shell devoid of joy or passion or hope, his spirit broken by the horror. War had stolen my Max from me, and it was a stranger who'd come home, now an absent stranger, who left a miserably small hole in my life. It was my Max I mourned in the wee hours.

As the boys grew, there were still hockey games to take them to in winter, tennis in the summer, and the beach whenever it was warm enough, all with Raymond sitting up front next to me, cheering his beloved brothers on. He'd lived more than three times what the doctors quoted, and they attributed that to me. But I was nothing special – wouldn't any mother do it for their son?

When he was twenty-seven, pneumonia took him suddenly. My grief for Raymond consumed me for a time. Without sharing it completely, I understood Max's broken spirit at last, but I refused to let my healthy boys grow up without me. I smiled when they went off to their dances, straightening ties and slicking hair and all those jobs a mother was meant to do, I supposed. But I felt like a shadow, without true joy or hope in anything for the longest time.

My sobbing barely woke me, but I was distantly aware of dear Annabelle's gentle fingers stroking my hand, my hair, my face, dabbing the tears that threatened to choke me until I drifted back to my fitful sleep.

Eventually, Robert fell in love. A lovely girl joined the family, but they soon moved away, though not too far. When Ronald found his partner, they left as well, with a promise that they'd be there for me if there was anything I ever needed.

And they were. Those sons of mine took care to see me often. They helped me move to a smaller unit, and paint it when it needed painting. When their babies came along, they made sure I was included in the birthdays and the milestones, the babysitting and the school events. And I began to heal from all my losses. I felt restored and hopeful once again, the shadow dimming, the light of who I was shining brightly once again.

Until they got job offers interstate.

I didn't want to stop them. I wanted all the best for them. Success. Prosperity. Fullness of life. Advancement. More. I took a lesson from my Raymond and smiled and waved and cheered them on when I knew I couldn't join them, as they left me all alone once again. Holding on to memories. Holding back the tears. Trying desperately to let go of the broken promises they'd made.

The years went by and there were visits each way, until, after my retirement, Ronald offered to have me stay. He built a granny flat for me and moved me in with all my gear. It was hard to leave my Max and Raymond, but I forced myself to focus on my living family, and the weddings coming up too soon among the grandchildren.

Ronald was a busy man, important, stressed and valued. I was happy for him, but hardly saw him. Robert would have me stay at his place whenever he could spare the time to come and get me, since he lived six hours away. He'd been divorced and remarried more than once, and his current wife didn't seem to like me, or having me in her fancy house.

I couldn't take any more remembering. Yes, there were the good times, watching the grandchildren become parents, seeing promises made and kept, though not to me or by me anymore. No, I'd given up on promises long ago. They only led to disappointment, anger and despair, especially when so many promised, and so few were really there.

I forced myself to stay awake, to chase the memories away. It was night, and yet dear Annabelle remained, breathing steadily in the chair beside me, still holding my good hand. Her other hand gently stroked her belly, and for the first time this visit, I became aware of the little bulge beneath that tender touch, giving away her secret as she slept.

She'd promised she'd stay right here with me, and she'd been true to her word, despite the boredom of sitting with a sleeping, ancient lady. Despite the trauma of seeing me so restless and so messy, both physically and emotionally. Despite my being mostly unresponsive all the time. And despite her own need for rest and sleep and food and bathroom breaks due to her now disclosed condition. Her secret. Her second promise.

For in that much loved little bulge was the promise that life would go on. I wouldn't be there to see it, but my family would endure. I'd somehow managed to triumph through trial, trouble and tribulation. My spirit had prevailed, bruised and battered but unbroken by desertion, disappointment and disease. I'd stood strong, and now could pass that strength to a new generation.

My unseen legacy.

One final promise for a dying old woman named Ada.

'Swift to its close ebbs out life's little day
Earth's joys grow dim, its glories pass away
Change and decay in all around I see
O Thou who changest not, abide with me'

From the hymn *Abide with Me*
by Henry Francis Lyte

Frank's Battle

Long ago, before technology reduced our existence to myriad collections of 280 characters, before tweeting became something presidents and teenagers had in common, instead of what birds do, Frank went to war. Posters promised world travel and adventure. Trudging through rubbled towns in France became an adventure in survival for Frank.

He spent his days in muddy trenches, edging forward, falling back, watching men who had become his brothers die. At night, moans of wounded soldiers echoed through no man's land, rousing weary men to retrieve the injured in the dark.

Sleep warped daytime horrors into nightmares, haunting Frank and fuelling the fear he fought with every breath. He huddled with his mates against the bitter cold, telling stories from home to stay awake. Knowing they were in it all together was the only thing that seemed to help. These blokes would be forever bound together by the secret dreadfulness they'd shared. Who else but them could ever understand?

Clouds crept across the firmament, promising rain that so often back home meant hope and broken drought, but here meant only more mud, mould, cold, and death. It didn't stop shells flying through sodden skies with dawn's light. One found its target, bringing Frank to his knees in freezing mire. His moan joined the symphony of anguish as many waited. Finally, stretcher-bearers took him to a field hospital, where doctors saved his life…

…but took his leg.

It had taken courage to climb out from the trenches every day, to shoot German soldiers as young and frightened as he was. He'd need more than courage to face the ever-present agony. The loss. The humiliation of life without his leg. Not even his mates could help him now. Frank fought a very private battle, building endurance and resilience with each and every day he faced.

His voyage home held only grim anticipation. No adventure, only grief. Frank used the time to build a place inside him. A place to stuff the horror. No one could comprehend the truth of his war story. No one knew the depth of pain that seared his soul. No one deserved to know, and suffer for that knowing. Capturing his memories would make the freedom they'd all fought for richer, or so Frank firmly believed. It would be hard enough to face the future legless.

His wasn't the ultimate sacrifice, mind you. He'd only lost his leg, not his life. Although sometimes he wondered which was worse – laying forever in a grassy field of remembrance, like John, or Tom, or Bill, or living unable to forget, without his leg.

How would he go on, he wondered?

Until he spotted his wife and son on the wharf and knew he'd have to find a way. War had grown within him the courage, the endurance, the strength he'd need for such a task. With the mates that were left he'd face one more struggle for survival in a world altered from the one they'd left behind – one that sold their youth and innocence for so-called freedom. Only time would tell the soundness of that deal.

But when he held Patricia in his arms and heard her whispered love between the tears, he knew he'd found the reason that he needed to face the battle to fit in. This time it wasn't freedom that he'd fight for – it was family.

With age comes... time

Older people can't help but have a unique perspective on time.
After all, they've lived for a long time.
They understand better than anyone how quickly time flies,
how rapidly things change, how important it is to use time wisely.

In one sense, older people have more time than young people.
Most of them have retired from paid work, and can now enjoy the
freedom to do whatever they like, be it volunteering, travelling,
pursuing hobbies or nothing much at all.
Some may even say they have nothing but time.

On the other hand, older people have less time than
most young people, in the sense that their time left on earth is short.
This could produce any or all of the following: anger, sadness,
regret, urgency, desperation, relief, recklessness,
determination or resolve.

The best thing we can do with this dilemma?
Don't rush.
Don't be in a hurry to get the visit over with.
Give them the gift of quality time,
because even though they have all the time in the world,
their time is fast running out.

Does Getting Lost Warrant an Incident Report?

'What would you like to do today?' Sally asks Joan on a beautiful sunny afternoon about five weeks into the Corona Virus lockdown.

'Well, I'm sick of these four walls, and my own company,' Joan says without a smile. 'Let's go out. I've got a letter to post. Where do you think we should go?' She turns it back to Sally, her Home Support Worker, to decide, which in itself is quite unusual. Joan is one strong-willed woman, who generally has a plan made before Sally even arrives.

Sally's superiors had recently complained when she'd clocked up eighty kilometres on an outing with this client. This, together with the general pandemic climate of limiting outings, prompted Sally to suggest posting the letter at the box just outside the retirement village, then buying take-away drinks from a local café. They could sit on a bench just down the road, overlooking the seashore. Plenty of tourists drive a long way to do just that, when the state isn't in lockdown.

'Too close,' Joan argues. 'I need to venture further afield. And that post box clears at noon, so we've missed it already. This letter has to go today.'

'How about we see if Bob's Place is open for takeaway, and find a park to sit in?' It's a fifteen-minute drive down the coast and Sally knows how much Joan loves Bob's Place. She was married to a Bob for nearly seventy years before he died ten years ago. It was one of her regular haunts with all of her carers. As added incentive, Sally finishes with a cheery, 'The sunshine is beautiful today.'

'No, we go there all the time...I know! Let's go to Finniss!'

'Isn't that a long way? They don't really want us to go too far, you know, with this virus business,' Sally isn't good at confrontation, especially with such a determined lady.

'Well,' Joan says, 'we won't be in a crowd or anything. And besides, I'm going stir-crazy staying at home.'

Sally recalls a recent reminder to take special care of clients' mental health during lockdown. And, of course, her training taught her the importance of respecting her clients and their need to feel in control of the care they receive. She also wanted every client to trust her to always have their well-being and choices as her top priority. Letting Joan have her way seemed to tick all the necessary boxes.

Now all she had to do was find her way to Finniss.

Joan seems somehow aware of Sally's hesitation and chimes in with a cheerful, 'My sister used to live in Finniss. I'll show you the way.'

Sally can't help but wonder how long ago that was. After all, Joan is in her 98th year, as she likes to put it.

As they drive, Sally begins to realise she's been hoodwinked. Joan talks about going by taxi to the hairdresser, yesterday. And to the chemist, the bank and the supermarket late last week. That's at least two outings since Sally took her out for coffee down the road last week. And then to the supermarket the following day, because she needed to shop in person, she'd said. She's hardly house bound.

After fifteen minutes on the road, Sally slows down for a turn-off she knows leads past a winery to Finniss, although the sign doesn't say that.

'No, not this one,' Joan orders, 'I'm sure it's further on than this.'

Sally's fairly confident there are numerous roads to Finniss off this main road, and Joan's enjoying being the tour guide, so she speeds up again.

After a while, they approach a sweeping bend with another road going off to the right. There's a big green sign pointing to Milang and Clayton. Sally feels certain they can get to Finniss down that road, but again Joan says, 'Keep going. There must be another road. We don't want to go to Milang.'

Further into the bend, a smaller sign says 'Finniss,' and, despite Joan's continued protests, Sally slows down and makes the turn. She's convinced they can find Finniss, then circle back on the winery road, minimising the kilometres whilst still doing Joan's bidding.

Sure enough, they soon come upon the Finniss General Store and buy a coffee and a custard slice each. In the absence of clearance details on the post box, Joan opts to look elsewhere to post her letter. Sally explains, again, why they can't sit in the dining room, or at the tables and chairs provided outside.

'But there's no one else here,' Joan argues.

'It's just the virus rules,' Sally counters.

'The problem is the fat between my ears,' Joan mutters when it finally registers that this is something she was aware of, as a global issue rather than a personal slight. 'It's solidifying.'

'We'll find somewhere nice along the way,' Sally says as she helps Joan back into the car, although she's no longer sure where they're on their way to.

Sally starts turning back the way they came, but Joan says, 'No, not that way. Let's see what's down this direction.'

The first time they come across a turn-off, there's no signage. Unfortunately, Sally left her familiarity with this area back in Finniss. The right fork in the road turns to dirt within their sights, and her co-driver/navigator advises, 'Stick to the paved road, Dear. No need to take us on the dirt.'

'Perhaps we'll end up in Mt. Gambier,' Joan says later, after telling Sally her family history, again.

Sally can't confidently argue otherwise, so she says nothing.

After what seems like forever, they come to a T-section. Milang is apparently two kilometres to the right, Strathalbyn sixteen to the left.

'Let's go to Milang and sit overlooking the lake,' Sally suggests, certain she can still find the winery road and get them back on track homeward. 'Be nice to have our coffees soon, before they get cold.'

For whatever reason, Joan still doesn't want to go to Milang, and makes that very clear, saying, 'I'd rather pull over and park on the side of the road overlooking the farmland than go to Milang and look over the lake.'

Sally turns left.

Every time she suggests a possible spot for their picnic, Joan turns it down. Their drinks are surely cold by now. Their custard slices warm.

Sally's hot.

And hungry.

And worried about the kilometres.

Finally, she just pulls over in a little-used driveway, just far enough past the 'bags of chicken poo $5' sign so she can have the window down without a stench.

Sally soon discovers there's quite an art to eating a custard slice in the car whilst conducting oneself in a professional manner. Fortunately, none ends up on her shirt, and she has tissues enough that she can use a few and still have some to offer her rather refined client, who seems to be really enjoying her afternoon tea.

Another glance at the clock and Sally feels enormously relieved the drink is barely lukewarm. She can skull it down and get back on the road sooner rather than later. They're more than halfway through their time, and she has no idea where they are. However, proper ladies in their 98th year do not skull a drink, and Joan makes it clear that she doesn't want to drink it going along. Sally reminds herself once again that it's all part of giving the client choice, treating them with respect, and helping them feel in control, then tries not to look at the clock anymore while she waits.

Finally back on the road, another ten minutes go by without seeing more than the odd farmhouse. Then Sally spies an 80-speed zone sign. Surely it must be Strathalbyn. If she can talk Joan out of stopping, they might just make it back in time. She begins to relax ever such a tiny bit.

Until she gets close enough to read the town announcement – Willyaroo.

She's been a local all her life, but had NEVER HEARD OF WILLYAROO.

'My brother used to live in Willyaroo,' her annoyingly unflustered passenger tells her. 'It was a red-roofed place, I think.'

Sally doesn't offer to go out of her way to look for it. The only road she's looking for is the one that will take them home.

After many more agonising minutes, and kilometres, they come into Strathalbyn. Finally, Sally knows where she is, even if it is still a monstrous forty minutes from home.

And yet another forty kilometres!

'Can we find the Post Office, Dear?' Joan's question indicates priorities far different from Sally's.

'I'm going to the Post Office back home after work,' Sally fibs. 'I could post it for you there.'

Thankfully, that appeases Joan.

It's a sober ride home. Sally's eyes spend equal amounts of time scanning between the road, the clock and the odometer. They're so far over the recommended 'don't go far' limit it's not funny, but there's nothing she can do. She has to get her charge home.

They turn into the retirement village at last, over-time as well as over-distanced. Joan seems almost repentant to a tense and weary Sally, until she says, 'Would you mind detouring round the lake so I can collect my mail on the way?'

And of course, not being one to argue, and still striving to achieve respect, trust and that feeling of control for Joan, Sally does just that.

Sally's stress levels are high that night when she thinks about notifying the office of her adventure with Joan. She fancies herself as something of a writer in her spare time, so sits down and debriefs into a story, pretty much like the one you've just read.

The following day, she times her visit to the office for mid-morning, and presents her superior with the story and a fresh mug of coffee.

'Enjoy a little read over morning tea. I'll be back with my timesheet later,' Sally calls as she hastily leaves the building.

When she drops her timesheet onto her boss's desk later in the day, Sally still expects a reprimand.

'I loved your story,' the boss says, then glances at Sally's 100km fuel claim.

'Is that all?'

'Aging is an inevitable process.
I surely wouldn't want to grow younger.
The older you become, the more you know;
your bank account of knowledge is much richer.'

William Holden

Poor Arthur?

Arthur rummaged through the linen cupboard, certain there was another blanket in there somewhere. He really needed to get everything out and put it all back in a more orderly arrangement, and maybe even toss a few things out, but that was not a job he'd tackle tonight. Tonight, he just needed another blanket, and preferred not to start stripping them from his bed if he could help it.

Finally, under a pile of... well, a mixed pile of towels and pillow-slips, he grasped a pink, fluffy thing he couldn't remember seeing before. It looked warm, regardless of its colour, and warmth was all he really cared about. He couldn't get it out without dragging the whole pile forward with it. Letting all the rest fall to the floor, he clutched his prize to his chest and hurried back to the lounge room. He only permitted himself two hours of telly each evening, and didn't want to miss the best shows sorting linen.

After turning off all the lights except the lamp in the corner, Arthur eased his stiff body into his armchair, tucking the blankets around his legs, adjusting his beanie, and grabbing the gloves Joan had made him all those years ago out of alpaca wool she'd spun herself. He prided himself on his routines, his systems, his repeated patterns of behaviour. They were the only reason he'd survived losing his Joanie. But he got to this point every night and never could work out whether to glove up first and then tuck the blankets up around his chin, or tackle it in reverse order.

He started each evening hugging a mug of cocoa. No need for gloves then, as the warmth from the mug soaked through his gnarled, achy fingers. He tried to get the gloves on fast after the last mouthful of drink left the mug quickly chilling, so as to capture the final remnant of heat. But the house seemed extra cold tonight. He'd gotten distracted with a crossword and hadn't closed the curtains early enough to keep what little heat the sun had provided from escaping through the glass.

Hence the extra blanket.

He put one glove on and tucked with the bare hand, which he left bare to change channels after the news. At seven-thirty, precisely two hours after he turned it on, he switched the telly off. Some of the advertised programs sounded interesting, but with the cost of power these days, he'd manage without them. No great loss, really. Not when he had a good book from the library.

As the evening wore on, he moved the book closer and closer to the dull glow from the lamp behind him. His son told him about some new-fangled LED globes, but he had half a dozen more of the old sort left in the laundry cupboard to use up first. If he was still alive when they were finished, perhaps he'd look into LED.

When the words became a blur, Arthur took the torch from the coffee table in his ungloved hand, turned it on and the lamp off, and proceeded to the bedroom. If only he could do the next bit really fast. His ninety-year-old joints just wouldn't co-operate with his desire for a quick change. Some nights, he wondered why he even bothered. What would be the harm in sleeping in his clothes anyway? They were nicely preheated with body heat.

Settling for a compromise, and moving as quickly as possible, Arthur took off his outer layer and put flannelette pyjamas, trackies and a wool jumper over the long johns that retained at least some of their warmth. He wasn't sure if it was the bulk of so many layers, or the arthritis, but he struggled to bend far enough to change his socks. Joanie would be horrified if he dared wear his day socks to bed. Come to think of it, she'd be horrified to see him suffering from the cold like he was. But thinking such thoughts didn't bring her back, or make living without her any easier, so Arthur changed the subject in his mind.

He climbed under the blankets and wiggled and jiggled until some of his warmth rubbed off on the sheets, then settled in to sleep.

The next day followed the pattern of so many before it. Arthur stayed in bed until his bladder screamed for relief. After seeing to that, he gathered all he needed and went for a shower, using the suction egg-timer he'd found at the Two Dollar Shop during the last drought to help him resist the temptation to linger under the hot water long enough to wash away the nocturnal stiffness. The steam barely had time to take the chill off the room, but he was grateful for every morsel of heat he could capture. He dried off fast and donned clean clothes.

His National Service callisthenics came in handy these wintry mornings, although some of the finer points blurred in his memory, and some allowance had to be made for his age and restricted movement. Who was he kidding? His sergeant wouldn't recognise this haphazard display of shuffles and jerks accompanied by numerous grunts and groans as anything even slightly military. But they did the job of increasing his mobility, and the added body heat was a welcome bonus.

In the kitchen, Arthur added exactly enough water to the kettle to make porridge and coffee. He'd measured it. No point heating any more than he needed.

After breakfast, he tackled the linen cupboard. It was nice to have something to occupy himself with. Kept his mind off the cold. Off his general state of misery. Off his loneliness. And trip after trip from passage to the kitchen table, where he tried to build piles of like linens, kept his body both warm and limber.

He started on the upper shelf, pulling as many things down as he could reach, knowing his family would be extremely upset with him if he climbed up on anything. In fact, Richard, his oldest son, had confiscated his handy little steps, taking them home with him after his last visit, so he'd have to use a chair. Even he realised that plan was fraught with danger. He blindly pulled handful after handful of random stuff, letting them fall to the floor.

He turned and looked at the messy mass. Lace doilies Joanie had made before they were married. His and Hers bath towels they got as a wedding present – they wore them out many decades ago, but Joanie was ridiculously sentimental, and didn't have the heart to toss them out. Placemats embroidered with pink and purple flowers – they'd never used them, but Joanie's favourite aunt Esther made them, so they kept them. Then he spotted something vaguely familiar. Delving amongst the stuff he'd likely toss, he unearthed a hidden treasure – better than gold. A hot water bottle, snug in a stripey cover Joanie had knitted the winter she was waiting for Richard's birth.

'Whooeee!' Arthur couldn't help letting out a yelp of delight, even though there was no one there to hear him. He'd be warm tonight.

Just as suddenly as the cheer had erupted, tears streamed down Arthur's cheeks. He had a flash of vision, whether remembered, imagined or some ethereal mystery. He saw his beloved Joanie beaming with satisfaction. Because even now, she was still able to look after her dear Arthur.

Using the well-worn hanky one of the kids had given him for some long ago Father's Day or birthday, Arthur wiped his face and blew his nose. He was lucky to have any such old faithful items left. He called them soft and worn-in, comfortable and kind to his old skin. His daughter, Katherine, threatened to throw such items out if she found any lying about when she came to visit. Since it involved the majority of his wardrobe, Arthur made doubly sure all the washing, drying and folding was up-to-date and neatly hidden away before she came.

Startled to discover it was well past noon, Arthur headed to the kitchen and boiled exactly enough water to make a cuppa-soup and a cup of tea. He put two slices of bread in the toaster, and cut four slices of cheese, as thin as his shaky hands would allow.

Arthur dragged lunch out as long as he could, steeping his old body in the sun coming in the dining room window, warming him on the outside, as the soup and tea did from the inside. This room was his favourite place to be on a winter's afternoon, with whatever sunshine there was flooding in. After two o'clock, he could walk down to his letter box and collect today's paper, a hand-me-down from the guy up the road who kindly left it there when he'd finished reading it in his lunch break.

Of course, today he had a particular ulterior motive for lingering. He was avoiding having to deal with the piles of linen covering all but the small corner of table he'd cleared with a hearty push as he arrived with his soup. He was sick of linen.

The phone rang.

'Aahh, saved by the bell, as they say,' Arthur muttered with a smile at his own small attempt at humour, partly amused at himself and partly concerned that, once again, he was talking to himself.

Hanging up the phone ten minutes later, Arthur couldn't help but release a long sigh, maybe closer to a groan. It wasn't that he wouldn't be thrilled to see Christopher, his youngest son. Or even that he wouldn't enjoy living a little less...well, frugally than he usually did. It was more the huge amount of work involved in hiding, well, no, let's say obscuring the fact that Arthur lived rather sparingly while no one else was here.

Not to mention the expense involved!

He'd have to put away all the extra blankets, from his recliner and his bed. And find the remote for the air conditioner. And remember how to use it. And stow the suction-egg-timer from the shower. The measuring jug next to the kettle would have to go, too. He'd also need to dust off the clothes dryer, plug in his electric blanket and stock the pantry with something more than Cuppa Soup.

He was exhausted just thinking about it.

Good thing Chris had given him plenty of notice. He'd keep up his thrifty lifestyle for four more days, and, of course, finish the linen project, then rip through the change-over the day before his son's arrival. They'd all be furious to know how miserly he was with himself. Arthur knew it was because they loved him, but it was really none of their business how he lived when he was alone.

And besides, the feeling was mutual – the love that is. That was the driving force behind his penny-pinching.

His parents and siblings had always lived carefully. Most of his generation had, having grown up through the Depression, and then the war. Things were tight. Necessities were hard to come by. Luxuries as rare as hen's teeth. Not that they were miserable, mind you. They learnt to have happy times without extravagance. Made their own fun without expense.

Until his mother died. The budget didn't change, but the happy times and fun evaporated faster than water spilt on the front porch in January. His father started drinking most of his hard-earned money, and gambling the rest, with little to no success. Arthur, being the eldest, got a job real quick, even though he was barely fourteen. It was a great relief as each brother grew old enough to join him winning bread.

He'd been married for a year, delighted to discover that living economically came naturally to Joanie too. In fact, she was even better at it than Arthur, and sure knew how to have a good time without expense. She made walks in the sunset, Sunday picnics and eating leftovers by candlelight seem like the most extravagant, romantic, special times. Memories he treasured to this day.

He hoped he might be able to spoil his darling Joanie a bit when his boss admitted he was ready to retire and suggested Arthur might buy him out of the electrical shop over several years. He'd be a business owner then, rather than just an employee.

But then Arthur's father up and died.

Other blokes he'd been to school with had got a helping hand to make a better life for themselves with money passed down from a relative of one sort or another. All Arthur inherited was a share in his no-good father's hefty debt.

Arthur shook the memories off, resolving not to pick up the burden of resentment he'd taken years to lay down. Without trying to, or knowing it, Arthur's dad had given him one useful legacy that made it impossible for him to be entirely ungrateful – something that drove every action Arthur took to this day. The rationale behind his modest lifestyle. The reason he didn't mind sleeping under five blankets, or having two-minute showers.

The determination not to be like his dad, and to leave something worthwhile for his children.

And their children.

And their children, too.

Although that night, as he discovered the hot-water bottle only really heated one spot in the bed, Arthur looked forward to a few nights with the electric blanket.

'All the world's a stage,
And all the men and women merely players;
They have their exits and their entrances,
And one man in his time plays many parts,
His acts being seven ages. At first, the infant,
…Then the whining schoolboy,
…And then the lover,
…Then a soldier,
…And then the justice,
…The sixth age shifts
Into the lean and slippered pantaloon,
With spectacles on nose and pouch on side;
His youthful hose, well saved, a world too wide
For his shrunk shank, and his big manly voice,
Turning again toward childish treble, pipes
And whistles in his sound. Last scene of all,
That ends this strange eventful history,
Is second childishness and mere oblivion,
Sans teeth, sans eyes, sans taste, sans everything.'

William Shakespeare
(Jaques in *As You Like It*. Act 2, Scene 7)

Tom's Understanding

June 1944, somewhere in Europe

The letter slipped from Tom's hand and fell to the floor without him even noticing, his face as impossible to read as the letter must have been – a jumble of emotions from anger and sadness to unbelief and shock.

'I thought we had an understanding,' he muttered to himself.

He and Violet had grown up together. You could say they'd slept mere inches apart, separated only by the party wall between the adjacent terraced houses their families rented in Becontree. She complained about his snoring. He knew she cried in her sleep.

They went to the same school, swapping sandwiches at lunchtime, and helping each other with homework. Tom was a whizz at math, and Violet could spell better than anyone Tom knew. When it came time for school socials and whatnot, Tom never thought of taking anyone but Violet. Conversation had always been easy between them, but that first time Tom pulled Violet close on the dance floor and they swayed as one to the music, his mouth went dry. He jammed it shut for fear of sounding as stupid as he felt.

Tom joined up as soon as he was old enough. His unit shipped out last October. He'd written to Violet every week, remembering the smell of her hair, the sparkle in her eyes, and the softness of her cheek as he kissed her goodnight after that last dance.

She'd written regularly at first. He loved to hear the everyday titbits of civilian life in London. Normality. Home. It made fighting for his country more bearable. Reminded him of what he was fighting for.

Then Violet's letters came less often. And were filled with parties and dances and her work at the munitions factory. Well, not so much her work as what went on in the breaks.

And now this.

Violet was pregnant.

Unmarried and pregnant.

To someone other than Tom, obviously.

What sort of a lowdown scumbag would take up with a soldier's girl while he was off defending civilisation as we know it?

What sort of a girl would let said scumbag get close enough to…well, too close, especially when she had an understanding with that brave soldier?

Tom couldn't believe it. Wanted no part of it.

He kicked the fallen letter out of his tent. Trod it into the mud.

And walked away.

May 1945, English Channel
'Those white cliffs look mighty good.' Eddie slapped Tom on the back with one hand and grabbed the rail of the troop ship with the other. 'Is there a better site in all the world?'

'I can think of a few, actually,' Tom replied with a smile.

'Ahh! I know. You're hankering after an eyeful of sweet Rosie,' Eddie nudged Tom with his shoulder. 'Is she waiting for you at the dock?'

'No, she couldn't get off work. She'll come round to Dad and Mum's as soon as she can.'

'Sounds all very friendly and comfortable. But not very romantic.'

'I told you they get on really well. Mum wrote and said how much they love Rosie already. How much they've enjoyed her visits. How it's almost like having a daughter.'

'Sounds like they've got you married off before you even lay eyes on her.' Eddie did the shoulder nudge thing again, trying to get a rise out of Tom.

'And that's just fine with me. Rosie and me, we've got an understanding.' Tom knew he should thank Eddie, but the smug blighter was acting far too pleased with himself as it was.

It was Eddie who'd 'introduced' Tom and Rosie. Well, he'd given Tom her address and told him to stop mooning over Violet. Tom put it off for weeks, wavering between utter disbelief and wanting to either desert and go punch a certain scumbag or desert and marry Violet anyway. None of those options involved ever trusting another woman.

But then he realised how lonely he was. How much he missed being able to share his thoughts and dreams with someone. Sure, he was living in very close quarters with his fellow soldiers – way too close for his comfort most of the time. But most of them you wouldn't tell a thing to, much less anything personal.

So, he wrote to Rose.

And she wrote back straight away. She seemed genuinely interested in everything he'd written, as if she really cared. She was best friends with Eddie's girl, Iris, so she'd heard of Tom, and wrote that she was pleased to make his acquaintance. Cute!

Every time he wrote, she wrote back, sometimes two or three times in a week. They had a lot in common – they lived in the same neighbourhood, although Rose only moved there with her family a few years back. Rose loved going for walks, gardening, playing cribbage and dancing. Tom nearly lost his leg daydreaming about dancing with Rose instead of looking where he was going under fire.

After laughing and crying through dozens of letters back and forth, Rose shared her dream of getting married and having three children – a boy first, then two little girls. Tom smiled when he read that, knowing that was his dream too. She started visiting his family, who fell in love with Rose up close, like Tom had from afar.

He never went as far as writing actual words like 'love' or 'marriage', but they 'talked' about settling down. About sharing their future. About building a life together after the war. He was certain Rose understood what he meant. And it made him a better soldier, having hope. Having a life with Rose to look forward to.

Soon enough Tom was home in the terraced house in Becontree. London had done it tough during the war, and there were bombed-out buildings and debris all over. Mum made no mention of Violet, and Tom didn't think to ask. He paced. He tried to eat the lunch his mum had made, with all his favourites. He listened for every footfall and checked his watch a hundred times.

And then Rose was there.

She didn't knock. Just appeared in Tom's lounge room. Eddie had described her to him. His mum had written about her thick auburn hair. But no words could prepare Tom for her beauty.

He jumped up, amazed he hadn't spotted her coming. He'd hardly taken his eyes off the footpath all afternoon. He stood, paralysed by the sight of her. Her hair wasn't just thick and auburn. It was shiny and red, weaving around her face like strings of fire. She was a perfect height for dancing. And her eyes. Such pools of sparkling emerald Tom had never beheld.

Snapping out of it, Tom nervously put his hand out to shake hers. What an idiot. He wanted to sweep Rose into his arms and kiss her socks off, but in that moment, she seemed like a stranger.

She took his hand and moved forward to kiss his cheek, a shy smile gracing her full lips. Without a word, they moved as one out the door and away.

They walked for hours, her small hand tucked warmly into his bent elbow. Walking in silence, they savoured the feeling of being on the same sidewalk together. Then words spilled out of them both at the same time, cascading together into a tumult of expressed thoughts and memories. And then they were silent again.

They found a park and huddled together on a bench, the cold encouraging the snuggling Tom was too shy to initiate. They talked about everything. And nothing. About her work, and his journey home. About their children.

It was the most natural thing in the world when Tom dropped to one knee in front of Rose and asked her to become his wife. And it was the most natural thing in the world when she said yes.

But the kiss that followed? Tom and Rose's first kiss? That could only be described as super-natural.

August 2004, Adelaide, Australia

Tom leant heavily on his son, John, determined to give due honour to his beloved Rose one last time by standing to place a white carnation on her coffin. He vaguely remembered the funeral guy asking whether Tom wanted pink for remembrance or white for pure love. He wished he'd chosen pink now. These blooms weren't white enough.

He stood for a long time, hoping the truth would somehow sink into his frozen soul. He didn't even know how this had happened. As much as the doctors tried to explain, nothing matched what Tom knew. Rose hadn't said anything about being sick.

And that's what really irked him. His understanding of 'in sickness and in health' was that if she was sick, he got to nurse her, care for her, comfort her. She'd done it for him plenty of times. How many times had she made chicken soup and spooned it into him when he had the 'flu? She'd cut the firewood after he'd had his knee replaced and picked up after him each time he hurt his back.

Yet she'd denied him the chance to express his love in that way.

If he wasn't so numb, he'd be furious.

Every time he'd noticed her looking peaked in those last few months, he tried to fuss. He asked what was troubling her. She denied feeling unwell. She went out a few times without saying where. Now he knew it was to see the doctor.

Then three weeks ago, he'd come in from the garden and found her on the floor, unconscious. He never saw her awake again. John and his two sisters came, taking it in turns to take Tom up to the city, to the big hospital's ICU.

Where they sat. Tom held Rose's hand, stroking his thumb over the papery skin. They said she could hear him, so Tom told her how much he loved her. How much he wanted her to get well so they could go home, together. How much he needed her.

But there was no response. No squeeze of the hand. No flutter of the eyelid. Nothing.

It got harder and harder to keep going every day. But impossible not to.

Then, as they were leaving home one morning for the hour-long trip, the doctor rang. This would be the last trip. This morning Tom would say goodbye to his beautiful Rose.

How could he do that?

He had an hour to prepare himself, but all he could do was remember his life with Rose. They were married within a month of his return from war. Why wait when you both know it's right? They moved into a terraced house right next door to Eddie and Iris and oh, what fun they had. Going to dances was their favourite pastime. Holding Rose in his arms was like heaven on earth to Tom.

Soon enough, their first child was born, a boy just like the dream they'd shared. John was followed by two girls, Nancy and Susan. Each time, Rose and Iris were in hospital together, with Tom and Eddie slapping each other on the back and exchanging cigars while the ladies recovered.

Tom thought he loved Rose before but watching her as the mother of their children multiplied his feelings a hundred-fold. The way she cared for those children. And the way she still found time and energy to do those special things for Tom thrilled him.

Tom remembered the day he arrived home all those years ago with an idea he'd seen on a pamphlet at work.

'Now Rose, what would you think about moving to Australia?'

'Isn't it half way around the world, Tom?'

'Well, sure it is, but they're desperate for workers and I'd be able to get a better job. We'd be able to afford a bigger place. Australia's full of wide-open spaces. And adventures.'

'It's a mighty long way from our parents, Tom. Our kids wouldn't know their grandparents.'

Rose looked worried, until they heard squeals from next door. The next moment, Eddie and Iris and their brood bubbled into Tom and Rose's place, announcing that they were off to Australia as 'ten-pound-poms'. That was enough for Rose.

'Us, too,' she chirruped, jumping and clapping along with all the children.

They'd sailed together and found houses in the same street. Tom and Eddie got jobs at the same plant. The children went to school together. They holidayed together. Who needed real cousins and aunts and uncles when the two families had each other?

They'd been there for each other through some rough times too. Iris fell into a deep depression after miscarrying twice. Tom saw a whole new side of Rose, staunchly standing by her friend.

She did it all again just recently, when Eddie passed away. How Rose's heart ached for her friend. She'd slept several nights with Iris, making sure she was all right. She'd brought Iris home for meals. Included Iris in everything they did. When Iris was finally able to spend a night at home alone, Rose talked long into the night telling Tom how important it was to her to help Iris without seeming to pity her. She kept talking until Tom said he understood.

As John's car approached the hospital, Tom wished he hadn't shushed Rose as she prattled on into another night. Fancy being so selfish. He'd give up sleep entirely just to hear Rose's voice again.

But there'd be no more sleepy conversations.

No more close, slow dancing.

No more laughing or love-making.

This was goodbye.

June 2005, Adelaide, South Australia

Tom still couldn't believe she was gone. If she was alive today, they'd be celebrating sixty years of marriage. How he loved her still.

Her clothes still hung in the wardrobe. Tom couldn't bear to part with them. On nights when sleep refused to come, when grief threatened to engulf him, he grabbed one of her dresses and held it close, imagining he could still smell her. He'd empty the wardrobe and surround himself with Rose tonight.

He picked up their wedding photo, and locked eyes with Rose, his bride, starring out of the frame. Her eyes held a cheeky sparkle, as if she had a secret. Tom remembered her leaning close as soon as that photograph was taken, whispering, 'I love you,' into his ear before brushing his cheek with a kiss.

Tom still thought he heard her whispering sometimes. 'Look after yourself,' she'd say, or, 'I love you, Tom.' Or, 'You're doing a great job with Iris.'

She hadn't said that last one for a while.

Not since he'd failed Iris.

After Rose passed away, Tom and Iris fell into a pattern. Mondays Iris cooked for him at her place. Wednesdays it was Tom's turn. He always did bacon and eggs for dinner. But eating anything with company beat eating alone.

Friday was fish night at the local pub. They went together and talked about old times. They shopped together. Shared a newspaper. Went for walks together.

They were friends with many shared memories. Tom would even admit to loving Iris. And he knew Rose would want him to. Because it wasn't the passionate, feel-it-in-my-bones kind of love a man has for a wife of sixty years. Tom and Iris were simply comfortable together. They both understood it would never be anything more.

Things got a whole lot less comfortable when Iris started showing signs of dementia. She'd tell him the same things twice. In a few minutes. She'd be forever losing things. She seemed, well, muddled.

Then, one day, Tom found Iris on his doorstep with a suitcase in her hand and a cheeky smile on her face.

'I'm moving in,' she announced.

'What?' Tom blathered. They'd talked about the practicality of sharing a house, to save on expenses. But Tom thought it was just talk. They'd have to jam two houses' worth of memorabilia into one. And what would the children say? Was this the dementia talking?

'I want to sleep in your bed tonight, Tommy.' Iris became more and more agitated as Tom went through all the old arguments with her. Then he thought of Rose and knew what he had to do.

'Okay, Iris.' He took her suitcase and ushered her in.

As Iris's condition deteriorated, Tom did more and more for her. He cooked her meals and washed her clothes. He did her hair and tried to take her places.

Tom's kids worried that it was too much for him. They must've hassled Iris's kids about it, because, after months of little contact, all three turned up to visit.

And took Iris away.

She didn't want to go. She cried and swore, and carried on like a right-royal banshee, although Tom was certain that was the dementia acting out. There was nothing he could do. They were Iris's kin. Her Power of Attorney. Her family.

They put her in a 'facility'. Somewhere in New South Wales.

They refused to tell Tom where.

Today he'd celebrate his sixtieth wedding anniversary. Alone.

The photo slipped from Tom's hand.

Tom curled up on the bed and wept.

If he understood one thing from his lifetime it was this. Love hurt.

October 2016, Flinders Medical Centre, Adelaide

Tom was dying. At last. It had been a long, slow process, starting when he'd failed his Rosie by losing Iris. He'd rattled around in the big house until the stroke. Then moved into an old folks' home.

He'd been lousy company all those years, letting the hurt rule.

But John and the girls still came.

He hoped they'd come back soon. He'd had lots of time to think, lying in this hospital bed, and he wanted them to know. He needed to tell them about his new understanding.

Love was worth it all. Worth the hurt. And the hard work. Love was worth everything.

'Life is like a roll of toilet paper.
The closer you get to the end, the faster it goes.'

Anonymous

Famous Last Words

Music echoed through the nearly empty house. Sarah couldn't understand how everything had been cleared out so quickly. And so thoroughly.

And yet there was music playing.

During all her growing-up years, there'd been music playing in this house. Country music. There'd been a portable radio on the fridge in the kitchen. Another on the mantelpiece in the living room. And still another on her mother's bedside table. Her mother may not have had an extensive record collection or a fancy turntable to play them on, but she made sure her favourite radio station, the one that played country music around the clock, was played where it could be heard in every room of the house.

But now her mother was dead.

'Come this way, Ms Harrington,' her mother's lawyer, Mr Hobbs looked overheated in his suit.

'Where did all the furniture go? What's going on here?' Not that she wanted the worn furniture. In fact, there was little belonging to her mother that interested her. Sarah had left this small town years ago to go to university and hadn't looked back.

Or been back.

They settled in the only remaining chairs, and Hobbs pulled a wad of papers from a briefcase.

'I have followed your mother's instructions to the letter, Ms Harrington.'

'I thought I'd have to go through everything, and deal with all Mum's… stuff. Still, it's wonderful you've done it all. Now I can get back to the city.'

'There is a box of things your mother wanted saved for you. She requested you look through it here. I'll leave you alone.' He stood and walked crisply away.

Sarah could still hear the music.

She picked up a photo album, wishing she didn't have to relive the childhood she'd worked so hard to leave behind. A dull family life in a dull little town. Never going anywhere or doing anything worth photographing. Her dad worked long hours to support them. Her mum made jam and stewed home-grown fruit, singing all the while, as if totally satisfied.

At the time, Sarah had thought they'd all been happy. Until she went to Uni. She rubbed shoulders with women who'd made something of their lives. Professors. Doctors. Scientists. Businesswomen. They didn't have time to make jam. They were making millions, making important decisions and discoveries. Making names for themselves. Just like Sarah had since then.

She opened the plain-covered book, which turned out to be more of a scrapbook than a photo album. Something fluttered to the ground. A newspaper clipping.

'Local singer heads to Tamworth,' the headline blazed above a photo of a woman with her guitar.

Her mother.

There were many similar clippings, dated over several years. Turning another page, Sarah found an ornately embossed invitation, yellowed with age:

'Miss Holly Easton
is invited to perform at the
Tamworth Music Festival Awards Ceremony,
Sunday, January 17th, 1978.'

Had her mother actually sung at Tamworth?

Why had she never heard about any of this?

She'd done plenty of singing while she washed dishes, hung clothes on the line, made beds and mopped floors. But Sarah had never heard her perform. Or heard of her performing.

She barely heard the hesitant knock above the country music. Sarah looked up at Hobbs, eyes full of questions.

'Perhaps you'll understand when you read this.'

How could the single page he handed her hope to explain so many secrets?

'I was more than satisfied. I was happy. And I'd do it all over again.'

Sarah scrunched the page against her chest and wept.

Then, blinking to clear her vision, she turned page after page of the scrapbook on her lap, desperate to see what her Mum had chosen over being a famous country music singer.

Clippings of her Mum's gigs gave way to copies of Sarah's school reports, graduation awards, and later, of articles Sarah had written, published in scientific journals. There were photos Sarah had sent her mum of award ceremonies, her nameplate on the door the first time she was allocated her very own laboratory, and other long-forgotten milestones in Sarah's career.

187

Nothing personal. No photos of her home, her pet, her holidays, because Sarah didn't take photos of such things. She didn't even have a pet. She'd shared so little of her life with her mum, but what she had bothered to send had been saved, cherished, preserved and celebrated.

Sarah turned the last page and picked up another album, craving a connection with the woman who'd given up so much to give her a stable, solid start in life. A start she'd always considered dull, but even more so now she was aware of all her mum had sacrificed.

She never really knew her mum. Her mum never really knew her.

And it was too late now.

She didn't want to leave this place. But there was no coming home now. The house was just that without her mum. A house.

She'd given so little of herself to her mum, who'd given all of herself for Sarah, and yet declared satisfaction, even happiness.

Sarah sat for a long time, pondering her mother's gift, while the country music played.

'Wisdom belongs to the aged,
and understanding to the old.'

from the Bible, Job 12:12 (New Living Translation)

The Best Summer Ever

'When do you leave?' I ask my best friend Noah as he crams books into his well-worn backpack.

'First thing Sunday morning. We leave home at 5.30 to be at the airport in time to check in. Then we're off to Sydney. After touring the Opera House and climbing Sydney Harbour Bridge, we take off for Bali.' I know he's not trying to rub it in. He is my best friend, after all. I know I should be happy for him.

'Sounds super,' is the best I can muster through my envy. 'Have a beaut time. See you.'

What an adventure. I've never even been on a plane before, and he gets to go on two flights. I run to catch up with William. Might as well walk to the bus with someone. 'I guess you're heading somewhere exciting with your family too?'

'Just to Queensland to visit my uncle. He lives near the Gold Coast. Imagine driving for three days stuck in the back seat with my two little sisters. *Aarrgh*! Great way to start a holiday.'

Sounds pretty good to me. 'Sure, but then you'll spend weeks lounging on tropical beaches and going to one 'World' after another.'

'Yeah, I guess that'll make up for it.'

Wishing him well as he boards his bus, I climb into mine and spot Ethan. He waves me into the seat beside him. 'What sort of

191

summer are you in for then?' I ask, dreading another tale of adventure and travel. Sure enough…

'My family's heading to Perth on the Indian-Pacific. We get to sleep in one of those pull-down bunks while the train goes all night.' I tune out what sounds too much like yet another summer adventure. 'How about you? Doing anything exciting for the holidays?' Nice of him to ask, I guess, but there's nothing nice about my answer.

'Just hanging out at my Dad's.'

Just as well Ethan's stop comes up and we part with a cheery 'See'ya,' cos I've had well and truly enough of hearing about everybody's plans for special family holidays.

I trudge home from the bus stop, dig through the rubbish in my pocket for the key and let myself in. Mum won't be home from work till 7, her note informs me. Time for a couple of hours on the X-box.

* * * * *

The train station bombards my senses as Mum drops me on her way to work, well before my train leaves. As she fusses around making sure I have my ticket and the key to Dad's place, I remind her that I'm fifteen years old, and it's only two hours in a train. I won't even be leaving the city. Just going from one end to the other. Some adventure that is.

'I'll miss you,' she gives me another hug. 'Ring anytime for a chat. If I'm at work, I'll have to call you back.' She treats her new job as if that's what makes her somebody. She used to be somebody pretty special when she was just my Mum, there for me every day when I got home from school.

'Yeah, Mum. I'll miss you too.' I hug her back. She clings a bit too tight and too long for a man my age to bear. I pull away. Enough mushy stuff. 'Don't work too hard. Have a great Christmas.'

Trains rattle in, spewing frantic travellers who all look as if they've got important places to be and should have been there hours ago. The crowd thins and I see a little old lady standing in their wake, looking as if she should be in a nursing home, rather than a crowded train station surrounded by a swarm of careless people.

She totters like a Tokyo tower in an earthquake, staring after a rather large parcel the human bees have knocked from her hands as they swarm on after the honey of success at any cost. I'm sure she'll keel over if she bends to pick it up, if knees that old can even bend.

I swoop in to snatch it up before she tries. Better a package to pick up than an old lady.

'Why, thank you, kind sir.' I stand a little taller at that. Not 'sonny' or 'young man,' but 'kind sir.' 'Very thoughtful of you.'

I grab her elbow with my spare hand to stop her sway from becoming a swoon. I lead her over to my bench and sweep my bag onto the ground so there's room for both of us.

'Does my hero have a name?' she asks, studying me with the watery, translucent eyes of the aged. I study her right back. The skin on her face looks so fragile, but the only wrinkles are laugh lines around her eyes and mouth. So, she's a happy old lady.

'Benjamin Taylor, Ma'am, but my friends call me Ben.' I hold out my hand and shake the thin, knobbly one she extends. 'Pleased to meet you, Benjamin Taylor. I'm Mrs Worthington and I'm ever so grateful that you came along when you did.'

Obviously still dazed by all the fuss, she adjusts her skirts and runs those well-worn fingers through her thin white hair. Just in time for another rush of people streaming out of the train that just pulled in.

'That's my train. Will you be alright?'

'I am truly blessed today. That's mine as well. Do you think you might extend your kindness further and help me get aboard?' She speaks so properly I could easily pass my English assignments if I had her help.

I collect her package and juggle my bag so that I've got a free hand to steady her, relieved that we seem to be the only ones getting on. Relieved, too, that we got up from the bench and got started towards the train early. A turtle would have no trouble beating her.

'*Aahh*!' she sits, patting the seat next to her in invitation. There's a whole train to sit in, but then again, she did call me 'kind sir,' so I settle our bags around us and sit next to her.

'Where are you travelling today, Benjamin?' She turns and smiles like she really cares.

'Going to stay with my dad for the holidays. All my mates are off on exciting family holidays, to other states and countries and I get to go across town to my Dad's.' Where did that outburst come from?

'Do you see much of your father?' She turns awkwardly in her seat. Could focussing on my face be more important to her than being comfortable?

'He and my Mum split up six months ago. I go there every other weekend, but he's pretty busy with work and, of course, there's always the girlfriend. His place is small, but I get a bedroom at least.'

'Good to hear you can see something positive in the situation. I'd guess your mother is pleased to have such a helpful young man to support her through what must be a trying time.'

Guiltily, I remember all the times Mum's had to nag me just to take my dishes to the sink, or put my clothes in the wash. I don't want to admit to Mrs Worthington that I could have been more helpful.

'Maybe.' I keep it vague. 'She's preoccupied with her new job and working out how to do all the things Dad used to do. That's what she says, anyway, when I try to get her to watch a movie or do anything with me. I don't know why it's so hard. Dad wasn't there much for the last year or so they were together anyhow.' There I go spilling my guts to a stranger again. What is it about this old dear that makes me think I can tell all? Maybe because she seems so interested.

She rests back in her seat, absorbed in her thoughts. I sit, mesmerised by the clickety-clack of the train as it jolts its way onwards. I smile at one of my favourite sounds as we whoosh past a crossing, the clang of the warning bell growing louder as we approach, then fading so quickly behind us.

'I suppose it's hard on all of you. Do you have brothers or sisters?' I can hear the understanding in her voice.

'No, it's just me. My mate William was complaining about sharing the back seat with two sisters all the way to the Gold Coast to visit his uncle. Doesn't sound so bad to me. Even sisters would be better than having no one to hang out with while Mum's at work. I don't even have any uncles. For years it was just the three of us for Christmas and birthdays. Now we're down to two.'

'I was one of seven children. Oh! We had some good times together. Lots of chatter and laughter at the dining table. Always someone to talk to. But, you know what?' She looks me straight in the eye. 'I'd have given anything to have my father or mother to myself sometimes, to have their undivided attention. I guess there's good and bad to every situation. We get to choose whether we dwell on the good or the bad.'

She's just beginning to sound like the school social worker getting warmed up for a lecture, when she changes track more smoothly than the train. 'Got anything special you hope to do in your time off school?'

Stalling, I take a look around. I get the strange feeling that admitting to really only wanting to sleep in, watch movies and play video games would disappoint her somehow, and for some unknown reason, I don't want to do that. I've been so engrossed in conversation I haven't even noticed the crowd growing as we near the city centre. Straphangers juggle the grab handles and their mobile phones, a lifeline in each hand.

'I'd have liked to make some money.' It's true, it just wasn't the first thing to come to mind. 'Pretty hard to get a job that only lasts till February, though. Dad will be at work all day. At least he's got plenty of internet. Guess I can download some shows.'

'There must be something better a smart young man like yourself can think of to fill his time.'

'What makes you think I'm smart? I've barely scraped a passing grade in most subjects this semester.'

'Yes, but what about before? You've been dealing with some serious changes in your life this last six months. Adjusting to it all will take some time. I remember when my Herbert passed away. It took ages for me to adapt. Suddenly I was living alone, sleeping alone, managing finances alone, and cooking meals for one. It was tough. The New Year's Eve nearly a year after he died, I suddenly realised that I couldn't live another year like the one that was ending. Herbert was gone and I was still alive. But I was hardly living. Right then I made the decision to embrace whatever was left of my life. Now I get out whenever I can, and look for ways to help others.'

The screech of the slowing train makes conversation impossible. We're in the city already. I have ten minutes to dash from this platform to the northbound side of the central station. Mrs Worthington starts fumbling with her handbag. 'Embracing life becomes difficult when packages are so much larger than you imagined.' She looks at me with a shy smile. 'Would I be imposing terribly if I asked my strong young hero to step in and save me once again? Lately I find catching the very next train impossible. I've taken to breaking the journey with a cuppa and some people-watching from the station café. I'd be delighted to shout you something in exchange for your help.'

She makes it hard to resist especially since the alternative is rushing to catch my train so that I can sit alone at Dad's. I gather her package up once again and head off down the aisle, then go back when I realise she's not with me. I forgot the turtle factor in any move she makes. I extend a hand to help her up. For a little old lady, she's got a mighty solid grip and I imagine I am a lifebuoy in the grab and pull of a rescue. 'Thank you again, kind sir. My joints get a bit stiff after such a long sit.' We walk down the rubbish-strewn platform like slow-motion robots.

* * * * *

Back on the train again, I am pleasantly surprised that Mrs Worthington is still travelling with me, and just as surprised that I find it a pleasant surprise. I also realise that waiting for a train has never been so entertaining. I'm usually pretty quick to find something to do on my phone to fill in any waiting time, but with Mrs Worthington around as my guide, the train station became a place equal to any tourist attraction. People from all over the world came and went, some in a hurry, some more relaxed. Together we tried to guess their stories, making up tales filled with such mystery and wonder I almost forgot my chocolate milkshake.

As the train rumbles out of town, she turns her focus to me once again. We talk about everything from pets to favourite school subjects and she seems to know all about current movies and authors and such. This is one well-informed, up-to-date old lady, yet she continues to be so fascinated by everything I say. 'What are you planning to do with your life when you've finished school?'

'I don't really feel strongly about anything yet. I wish I did. They want us to choose subjects and pathways and I just don't know.'

'What do you enjoy doing?' She asks question after question, but instead of feeling like she's interfering or just plain nosy, it feels like I'm seeing my future more clearly, and even imagining being successful and worthwhile. That's a first for me.

'Whatever you decide on, I'm certain you'll do it well, Benjamin. You seem an intelligent, sensitive and thoughtful young man who could succeed at whatever you put your mind to.' I blush with all those compliments. Is that really how she sees me? 'You'd have every reason to be confused and hardened by the stressful situation you've faced at home this year. The fact that you were willing to reach out to help an old lady in need, and be such a delightful companion to me, tells me that you are made of tougher stuff. I'm sure you have it in you to rise above your hardship and grow into a better man because of it.' She has more confidence in me than I do.

I don't know what to say to that. I realise that the silence is only in my head – the rhythmic clink, clink of the wheels on the tracks punctuates my thinking. She really does believe in me – the screech of the wheels as we come into a curve. She says it only matters that I do my very best at whatever I choose to do – the rattle-bang-rumble as the cars jostle northwards. I want to succeed just to prove her faith in me was well-founded – the high-pitched chant of the horn, swallowed up by the hiss and whoosh of the brakes signalling another stop.

My stop. Our stop. I realise that we've come to the end of the line and Mrs Worthington is still beside me. That was the shortest ever trip to Dad's. This lady is amazing. I feel like she's known me my whole life. She reaches for my hand. 'I'm sorry to say, but I need to impose on your gentlemanliness one more time to help me off the train, please Benjamin?' Her smile makes it impossible to resist her request.

Once again on solid ground, she extends her hand to shake mine. 'Thank you for keeping a lonely old lady company, kind sir. I wish you a happy holiday and a successful life.'

I wish I could hug her. 'I'd like to help you to your house. I'll carry the package for you if you like.'

Ambling along at her turtle-pace, I think about the amazing journey I've been on. Noah and William and so many others have travelled far and away to look at new things in new places. I stayed home and discovered a new way of looking at my life right here. A better way of viewing my life, my family, and my future.

I realise that while my thoughts were wandering into a brighter future than I had previously dreamed of, my feet were wandering along my Dad's street.

'That's where my Dad lives. Is your place close by?

'Well, actually Benjamin, it appears we are to be nearly neighbours for the summer. If you like, I'll check with your father tonight about you spending some time with me. You said you wanted to earn some money these holidays. How do you feel about mowing lawns and fixing a few things for an old lady? And maybe, if you don't think it would be too boring, we could play some board games? What do you think?'

I think I might have just found myself the sweetest ever stand-in grandma for the holidays, and hopefully beyond.

'I think that sounds like the best summer ever, Mrs Worthington. My Dad gets home at seven.'

With age comes... bucket lists

No matter how long we live, or how much we do in our lifetime,
there'll always be something more we wished we'd done.
And as the end of life draws nigh,
a sense of urgency to do certain things develops.

There are the frivolous, showy wishes that see ninety-year-old
ladies jumping out of planes, eighty-year-olds going
up in hot-air balloons,
seventy-year-olds climbing Sydney Harbour Bridge,
and, in my own case, sixty-year-olds feeding giraffes.

And then there are the deeper things, frequently
out of the older person's control. These don't often make it to
the public bucket lists, or the ones they make movies about.
It might be to see the last grandchild get married,
or the first great-grandchild safely born. It might be to make
a century and receive a birthday card from royalty.
Or see a son conquer cancer.

But if you take the time to ask, there might be something
less extreme, some achievable longing that you could help
make happen. A drive to the jetty where Grandad did his best
fishing back in the day. Fish and chips on the bench where
Grandma had her first kiss. Sorting through the heirlooms and
labelling who they're to be handed on to when she dies.

There's no telling how much more the older person might achieve,
how many tomorrows they'll have.
So, if you can, tick something off their bucket list with them today.

The Project

Glenn woke to the sound of his wife, Carol, fussing about the bedroom. He wasn't sure if she was trying to be quiet so as not to disturb him, or secretly wishing she would disturb him because she thought he was a lazy bum. After all, he thought he was a lazy bum, so why shouldn't she? With that in mind, he rolled over and pretended to be asleep. There was no reason to get up, anyway.

His alarm had been set for 6.30 am every week day for more than fifty years. And every week day for more than fifty years, Glenn had listened to the ABC news and weather before he got up. His morning routine was always the same – shower, shave, put on his dark grey trousers and one of the many blue striped shirts Carol faithfully ironed every Thursday evening. He'd match the shirt with one of the navy blue ties his kids dependably gave him for every birthday, Christmas and Father's Day, alternating with a steady supply of black business socks, of course.

Then he'd go to the kitchen, where Carol would have his coffee ready, his lunch packed, and his vitamins waiting next to a glass of water. He'd choose a breakfast cereal, except for a brief period in the 70s when they went through a yoghurt-and-fresh-berries phase. If he pushed the toast down exactly as he started on his cereal, it would pop as he swallowed the last mouthful. Perfect timing to eat it nice and hot, spread liberally with butter and honey in the early years, margarine and peanut paste when the kids were in school, and more recently, cholesterol-lowering non-dairy spread and vegemite. On those few brief occasions when Carol was away, Glenn would give a cry of, 'Let them eat jam,' and do just that.

By 8.00 am he'd be pulling into the carpark at work, an hour ahead of opening time. He'd always been there early, even before he took over ownership of the insurance and investment brokering company thirty-five years ago. There was always plenty to do to ensure the day ran smoothly once the doors were opened for customers. He'd been there the very first day they opened, as an apprentice to old Mr Simms, who had no sons. He trained Glenn to take over eventually, which was exactly what had happened.

Glenn had stayed long after he reached retirement age, not doing much in those last few years, of course, but he still had his finger on the pulse. He knew every client by name, every claim. He was in the same boat as Mr Simms, with none of his children interested in taking over, no matter how far past seventy he got, no matter how long he hoped and prayed his baby, his life, could be passed down to family.

In the end, with a certain sense of hopelessness he tried to deny, because it meant his whole life was a resounding failure, he sold it to his manager, Joe. Joe had always shown a great deal of promise, always been enthusiastic, genuine and kind to the clients. He'd look after it well. But he wasn't family.

Realising that lying there pretending to be asleep was only allowing his all too depressing thoughts to run rampant, Glenn got up. Not dressed, mind you, just up.

He wandered down to the kitchen in his gown and slippers. Perhaps they should start getting the newspaper delivered. Then he could find a sunny spot in the front room and sip coffee and read the paper, cover-to-cover, like all the retired blokes did in movies. Then maybe he'd do the crossword.

Oof! Who was he kidding? Snow would fall on Uluru before he'd be caught dead doing a crossword. If he lived as long as his Dad, God rest his soul, he had at least another twenty years in him, and he wouldn't be resorting to crosswords to fill them any time soon. Not that there was anything wrong with crosswords, and he certainly wasn't judging anyone who did them, but they simply weren't for him.

He was more of a Candy Crush kind of guy.

Rather than go searching the house for Carol, he poured himself a coffee and pulled out his iPad. She was most likely engrossed in one of her projects. She was always busy with something. He'd just have one game, then go say hello.

Two hours later, Carol flustered into the kitchen with an, 'Oh dear, I got carried away with my sewing and lost track of time,' followed by a quiet, as though she didn't want Glenn to hear it, 'Looks like I'm not the only one!'

He heard it all, including that exclamation mark at the end, accentuated by a raised eyebrow, no less. But it was 11.00 am. And he was still in his pyjamas.

Still, he refused to feel guilty. He'd worked hard all his life. He deserved to take it easy now the pressure of running a business was behind him. And, apart from any of that, there really wasn't anything else to do anyway.

What Glenn didn't realise was that there was absolutely no condemnation in that eyebrow raise, nor in the exclamation mark that had slipped out before Carol could contain it – not condemnation, but merely dismay, and perhaps, no definitely, a little sadness, that her always pulled-together husband seemed to have come adrift. And she didn't really know how to help him pull himself together.

August
Some days, Glenn arose with Carol, not at 6.30 am like they always had, but at the far-more-suited-to-retirement hour of 7.30 am. Those were the mornings that dragged the most. If he rolled over and dozed after she left the bedroom quietly, he could easily shave a few hours off the morning quota of emptiness he had to fill, somehow.

When he did rise, he put on his work clothes, just like always. Apart from his mowing-the-lawn jeans and flannel shirts, and, of course, his Sunday church clothes, that was all he had in the wardrobe. Carol had urged him to go shopping, then offered to go with him, then, in sheer desperation, offered to buy 'retirement clothes' for him without him. She also suggested he sort his work clothes ready to donate, then offered to help him, and finally offered to do it for him.

'I'm just not ready,' he'd replied every time, defensively standing guard in front of his wardrobe lest she take them away without his permission. Somewhat like the security blanket he'd clung to well into his Kindy experience, Glenn clung to those clothes. They gave him value. Because he'd worn them, he'd been somebody. Now, not so much.

He and Carol had slipped into a pattern of sorts. She would nearly always be busy with one of her projects by the time Glenn got up. If he felt brave enough, he'd track her down and take an interest, wondering if she noticed his pretence. He knew nothing of sewing, knitting or quilting. Cutting up perfectly good fabric into little geometric shapes so you could sew them back together and hang them on the wall seemed ludicrous to Glenn. But it gave Carol unending joy, so he gushed over the way she blended the colours, and delighted in her smile.

He had to be careful though. If he seemed too cheerful, or too interested, she'd make suggestions of things he could be doing with his morning. Glenn was certain she had a written list of Glenn-shaped projects memorized, because she never failed to come up with something – repot the indoor plants, sort out a box of photos, clean out the shed. He admitted they needed doing, but he wasn't ready to start any of those things yet. Then, for at least a week after she'd asked him to help cut out mauve floral triangles, he'd had to tone his greeting and interest down to a dull hello. Heaven forbid she ever again expect him to join her for longer than that in the sewing room.

The best days, and oh how he hated to admit it, were the days she had somewhere to go. It annoyed him, really, that her life was filled with such purpose, but he didn't say anything. If he wasn't careful, she'd invite him along. Mondays it was Meals on Wheels, but not until 11 am. On Wednesdays, it was her volunteer shift at the Op Shop in the morning. And Friday afternoons she went to quilting class. Not to mention her once a month on a Tuesday lunch with the women from church, and her fortnightly Probus meeting on Thursday mornings. He struggled to keep up, never too sure where she was going when she said her cheery farewell.

But he couldn't help the sigh of relief that escaped his lips as the roller door closed on her departure. She'd never know it. She was just doing what she'd been doing for years after retiring from her part-time retail job. She didn't realise that her busyness only made him feel worse. She wasn't doing it to rub it in. She wasn't calling him lazy or useless or a big, fat nobody because he had nothing to do and nowhere to go. He was putting that on himself. But at least, with her out of the house, he could lose himself in his Candy Crush and no one would know.

October
Carol was out, again, and Glenn, in one of his rare moments of motivation, took a stroll around the garden. Everywhere he turned, spring had worked its magic – the sky was blue, the rosebushes were covered in buds, the birds were singing. There was brightness and colour and potential whichever way he looked.

They'd had a plan, he realised. Their life had been a long journey on a fairly straight, narrow and well-thought-out set of tracks, to an anticipated destination. But somewhere towards the end, the train had derailed. Sure, he could put some of the blame squarely on the pandemic, since travel had been an important part of their retirement plan. They'd planned some caravanning, some cruising, and some long-range flights, but with border closures, and quarantines, it just wasn't worth trying any of it, and may not be for some time yet.

But travel wasn't all they'd planned, and Covid wasn't the only problem. Much of it rested squarely on Glenn's shoulders, or more likely just up from there. His head alternated between being fuzzy or thick or dull or dopey most of the time. He couldn't even focus long enough to watch a movie. He couldn't think through a sequence of actions and outcomes. He couldn't remember things. Until his stupid head hit the pillow each night. Then, suddenly, it was buzzing with thoughts, plans and ideas that kept him from sleeping.

He did nothing all day, but he was tired all the time.

And he was lonely. His days at work had been full of people. He not only knew their names, he remembered them, and their stories. Now, apart from Carol, the only human interaction he had was a handshake and a 'Howdy' with the minister on the way out of church on Sundays.

He realised, sadly, that he didn't have many friends. Sure there were some couples he and Carol got together with for a meal every so often, but, as far as mates go, he could count them on one hand. He'd never chosen to spare the time from work necessary to successfully propagate a friendship. Now, time was all he had. But he wasn't desperate enough to take to the golf course with Peter. Nor could he abide Ken's passion – fishing. Rob played bowls, but Glenn had always said bowls was for old people, and he wasn't prepared to admit he was there just yet. So the only connection he regularly maintained was with the kids and grandchildren, via phone calls or zoom sessions.

No amount of spring sunshine could stop the dark clouds from settling over his soul whenever he thought of the kids not wanting to take over the business. He was handing them a ready-made ticket to success, and all four of them said a big, 'No thanks, Dad.'

Glenn stood in the garden and gave himself the same stern talking to he'd given himself dozens of times already, trying desperately to convince himself that when they rejected his business offer, they weren't rejecting him. Not wanting to follow in his footsteps truly wasn't the same as calling his life a waste of time. After all, they'd had a good many good things in their lives because he'd put so much of his life into that business – orthodontics, private schools, air conditioning, interstate family holidays. He had to believe their dismissal of his life's work wasn't a dismissal of him, although most days it still felt like it.

He sat down on the patio and sipped his lukewarm coffee. Hah! His melancholy really had made a fool out of him. All this self-talk was unnecessary nonsense. He only had to look at the mug they'd given him for Father's Day last month, and remember all the kind words in the cards they'd sent to realise they were, indeed, full, not only of gratitude for all he'd done for them, but also respect, appreciation and love. And they were quick as well as eloquent at expressing it.

Perhaps his life wasn't a complete failure after all.

December 31st
On the wave of October's epiphany of value, Glenn had realised the benefit of getting outside. It was way harder to feel morose with the sun warming his skin, and nature in all its glory surrounding him. He found that he quite liked tinkering in the garden, and had even built a raised garden bed. His summer vegies were coming along nicely. Carol was ecstatic to support him in a project he'd thought of for himself.

He'd also discovered some nearby walking trails. Not hiking tracks, but gentle walks he could do without special equipment or training. After his first few expeditions, he felt so energised and encouraged, he invited Carol to join him. Those early walks together were quiet adventures into nature, but soon enough, they were chatting away like newlyweds, about all and sundry. Nothing too deep, but a beginning again, a sharing of old and new, a reinvention of things in common. Perhaps even a restoration of sorts, of a marriage by no means in trouble, but just a bit too comfortable, a bit taken for granted. He began noticing again what he should have seen all along – that his wife was a pretty terrific woman.

As they held hands and watched the New Year's Eve fireworks from their balcony, Glenn made an easy resolution – to spend more quality time with Carol. Not that he was signing up to learn to quilt. That would never happen. No, they'd always need their separate projects, so they had something to talk about when they were together.

As the blazes of colourful light dimmed, and the war-zone-like sounds of the roman candles and aerial spinners fell silent, the lingering remnant of metallic smoke clouded Glenn's mood. As nice as the refreshment of his marriage was, as much as he enjoyed walking outdoors and accomplishing little projects in the garden, winter would eventually come. Summer's sun would fade. He didn't want to fall back into the sour habits of those first few months of retirement.

He just didn't know how to stop himself.

April
As he changed the last of the clocks in the house back to non-daylight-savings time, Glenn realised that, whilst he'd finally regained the hour he'd lost last October, he'd lost his mojo, his spark, his zest for life. Well, actually, it had been a very long time since he'd felt zesty about anything.

His garden lay dormant. He still walked, but having to layer up already with coat and beany was getting tedious, despite autumn's mild start. He'd updated his wardrobe with what Carol deemed suitable 'retirement clothes' and donated most of his sacred work clothes to the Op Shop where she volunteered. He'd loaded them into the car for her one Wednesday morning, but couldn't bear to watch them drive away. Then he'd indulged himself, blowing his self-imposed limit of an hour of Candy Crush per day. He was still at it when Carol returned in time for lunch.

He'd tidied his shed so well, he could've eaten lunch off the floor, which he almost felt he deserved after slipping so far back into old, comfortable habits of despondency. He'd even sorted some of the photos into very orderly boxes labelled for each decade of their lives. There was much more to be done there, but he just couldn't get into it – looking back to all they'd done as a family, all the places they'd been, all the lives they'd touched only highlighted his current lack of…well, anything. He fell short in every area. He achieved nothing meaningful with each passing day. He went nowhere. He failed to impact anyone else. Instead of filling his mind with happy memories, those photos only served to remind him of the current emptiness of his life.

After lunch, Glenn headed off for a walk, turning down Carol's offer of company. He needed time to think. The clear blue sky leant a brightness to the autumn afternoon and with each deep breath Glenn let warmth permeate his cold soul. He needed a new project. Not a finite, physical project, but rather something lasting, something with meaning, something of value.

Glenn's pace began to slow and he realised he'd been so lost in thought he'd diverted from his usual level track to take a new path, leading to a steep climb. Determination drove him on, until he stood at the top, hands on knees and fighting to catch his breath. When he did, he stood tall, sucked in some deep gulps of salty air, and was awestruck by the coastal panorama before him. He'd never seen it from here before. He'd always taken the easy, flat path, through trees and open grassland, or along the sandy shore, avoiding the effort, but missing the reward of the steeper trail.

He stood gazing in all directions for a long time, captivated at every turn by the distance, the expanse, the beauty. And then he knew.

His new project would be taking the higher, harder path to completely reinvent himself. Not just taking Carol's suggestions. Not just wallowing in his own gloom. He needed to make an effort, to look beyond himself. To find something or someone outside himself that his gifts and talents could impact.

Glenn's new project was...Glenn.

'What we have once enjoyed we can never lose.
All that we love deeply becomes a part of us.'

Helen Keller

Really Old Habits Die Really Hard

James was a man of habit. He didn't consider himself boring. Just… regular. He'd done particular things in certain ways and they'd felt good. Right. They'd fitted his personality, his lifestyle, his day. Doing them hadn't hurt anyone, and even seemed to make those around him happy, so he found himself doing them again. And again. Until everything fitted into a nice routine that replayed itself every day.

He felt comfortable.

Settled.

Until this morning!

He reached out to start the day exactly as he had for the last seventy-two years. He loved the feel of his Barbara's hair, soft and smooth as he ran his clumsy fingers through it. He loved the way she snuggled into his side, warm and sleepy, as they moved from sleep to wakefulness as one. They'd always started the day together, no matter what it held.

Once they were both awake, they'd take a few minutes to share their plans for the day. To connect. Others they knew started their days with the radio news. Or breakfast in bed. But James and Barbara loved their morning banter. In the early years, it anchored them to each other ahead of a day of separate busyness.

And the habit stuck.

Of course, they'd had a lot more time together since James retired. They'd travelled. They'd visited family far away, and hosted various parts of their huge clan right here at home. They'd extended the garden, catalogued the photos, and kept up with what seemed like an enormous number of medical appointments.

Whatever different things they did throughout the years, certain things remained the same. For nearly fifty years, Barbara always had James's work clothes picked out and waiting for him on the bed when he came out of the shower. She knew just which tie went with which shirt, and which socks he liked to wear for the office, and which were better for weekends. She stroked his freshly shaven face and kissed the resulting smile.

While she put washing on, or finished getting herself ready, James started heating the milk for their oats. By the time Barbara entered the kitchen, he had the coffee made, the porridge in the bowls with a drizzle of golden syrup, and the newspaper on the table. Like synchronised swimmers, they moved through the breakfast ritual, neither missing a beat.

James read the sports section, while Barbara preferred the front pages, relating relevant or interesting news stories for him between mouthfuls. By the time he turned around after taking their dishes to the sink, she was waiting at the door with his hat and his packed lunch, her face turned upward for his farewell kiss.

Mornings hadn't changed much since James retired. He still shaved every day, just to earn the stroke and kiss from Barbara. The clothes she still insisted on choosing became more casual, but were always waiting for him on the bed. The dispensing and taking of medication had worked its way into the breakfast sequence, but all else remained the same.

Retirement brought new habits later in the day. Instead of sitting at his office desk with his sandwich and fruit, James raided the fridge while Barbara defrosted bread. In summer, they sat on the patio to eat. In winter, James lit the fire and they ate inside. Regardless of the season, Barbara ate with pen poised over the cryptic crossword from the paper, reading out clues around bites of her lunch.

All except on Wednesdays. That was the day they ventured out for lunch. It started years ago, when they decided to try a different local café every week. But they'd both fallen in love with Carol's Place, and didn't bother going anywhere else.

Every Wednesday, James and Barbara went to Carol's. James ordered a bowl of chips with gravy. Barbara ordered the chicken salad. The server provided two empty plates. James put half the chips on each, with less of the gravy going Barbara's way. Barbara put half the salad on each, with all the tomato on James's plate, and all the cucumber on her own. Perfection.

Evenings, also, were steeped in tradition. Barbara greeted him at the door each day of his working life, unless she was in hospital having one of their six children. He never settled for a welcome peck on the cheek, sweeping her into his arms for a long embrace. He wanted her to know how much he'd missed her. How much he appreciated the home she kept so beautifully for him to retreat to each night. How very much he loved her.

And no matter how busy she was, and boy did she get busy, with dinner preparations, supervising homework, sorting out squabbles and the like, she always made time for that delicious cuddle. His reward for a job well done at the office. Not that he needed more than the chance to come home to Barbara.

Even after he retired, he often found somewhere to go in the afternoon, just so he could come home and hug Barbara. He went to his mate Ken's for a game of chess. Or to the hardware store for any little thing. It didn't have to take long, or even be important. Just as long as it got him out of the house for a while. Even if he hadn't worked hard to earn their keep, it seemed, somehow, he always earned that wondrous embrace with Barbara before dinner.

Which was always eaten in the dining room. No TV dinners for them. They talked about their day. Communicated important issues. Shared trivial happenings. Laughed. Complained. Encouraged.

Then settled in the family room to watch TV while Barbara knitted tiny jumpers for the children. Then the grandchildren. And then the great-grandchildren. It was James's job to get the children off to bed, and make the hot milk and honey for their supper. It was the least he could do after all Barbara had managed all day. Once the children were grown, there were still the supper drinks to make, a book to read, or bookwork to do.

Like precision drivers at the car show, James and Barbara manoeuvred through the bedtime sequence, James turning back the covers while Barbara cleaned her teeth, then James doing his while she changed into the nightie he gave her every year for her birthday. Finally, one of his favourite parts of the day. He changed for bed while counting the one hundred strokes as Barbara brushed her hair. Hair that was thick and long and dazzlingly auburn when he first fell in love with Barbara, and was just as beautiful all these years later, when it was thin, and grey and wispy.

At the hundredth stroke, they'd snuggle into bed, finishing the day as it had started. Sharing memories and hopes. Together. In love.

And the routine would start all over again the following day.

Until this morning!

He reached out, anticipating the feel of Barbara's soft smooth hair as he had for the last seventy-two years. Only to find an empty pillow. There was only cold emptiness on her side of the bed. No one snuggled into his side, warm and sleepy.

James was starting the day alone.

In his sleepy haze, it took James a moment to realise what had happened. To remember the tragedy. There was no one to share his plans for the day. There were no plans.

He was adrift in a sea of sorrow.

James lay in bed far longer than usual. Being a creature of habit was the only thing that eventually got him moving, and his bladder, of course. But there were no clothes waiting for him on the bed when he came out of the shower. How would he decide what to wear? Did it even matter? Habit made him shave, but without Barbara to stroke his freshly shaven face and kiss his smile, he seriously wondered why he bothered.

He heated far too much milk for one serving of oats and threw the excess down the sink in disgust. Synchronised swimming doesn't work when you're in the pool alone, and James was all out of whack. The paper held no interest, he couldn't find his pills and he didn't know what to do next.

His son Peter arrived while James was still sitting at the table. He needed answers about the funeral. But for years now Barbara and James had spent the morning together, sharing the load of the household chores, muddling through the washing and the cleaning the way they'd muddled through life – together. James's need for order didn't allow for funeral planning.

James mumbled and fussed and tested his son's patience. Peter tried to hide his frustration until he found the folder his mother had set aside with instructions for such a time as this.

At twelve noon, James moved to the fridge, but his companion today wasn't Barbara, and Peter didn't know how to play her part. James stood in the kitchen, lost, until his daughter Jenny came with lunch, but it didn't taste right without the crossword. Nothing was the same. Nothing fitted anymore.

* * * * *

Three months later, Wednesday came around, again, and James once again faced a dilemma. Habit told him to head to Carol's, while his heart told him there was no point. Habit won! He ordered a bowl of chips with gravy…and the chicken salad. The server provided an empty plate along with a plastic take-away bowl. James put half the chips and half the salad on each, leaving all the cucumber right where it was. It was an uncomfortable change to the routine. One he'd come to terms with. At least he'd have dinner for tonight.

Jenny phoned, as she had every afternoon since Barbara's passing, suggesting James go for a nap after lunch. He'd never napped in the afternoon. But there was no point going out so he could come back home to Barbara. He really didn't like going anywhere. Not without Barbara. And not without Barbara's embrace to welcome him home. Home to her. Home was her.

But not anymore.

Some habits were simply too hard to manage without Barbara.

* * * * *

Six months after the longest, most awful day of his life, as James waited for the milk to heat for his supper, he knew it wasn't just because he liked hot milk and honey for supper. All the things he'd ever done in those particular ways he hadn't done because they'd felt good and right. He hadn't done them because they'd fitted, because they made him feel comfortable.

He'd done them because that's how he and Barbara lived.

And it was Barbara that made him feel good and right and comfortable. How would he ever live without her?

Maybe if he gave up on the habits, he wouldn't miss her so.

Still, after finishing his milk, James found himself turning back the covers and standing for a long time, at least one hundred seconds, staring at Barbara's side of the bed. She wasn't brushing her wispy, grey hair. And never would be again.

Yet every night he saw her there. And every night he waited for her to finish. Because even though the habits weren't the comfort in James's life, letting go of Barbara was the hardest thing he'd ever had to endure. He couldn't bear losing their routines as well.

So he did them all just as if she was here with him.

Because in the rituals, she was.

'If you always do what you've always done,
you'll always get what you've always got.'

Henry Ford

Chasing Shadows

I'm worried about Pam.

She's been my wife for nearly forty-five years, my best friend for more than fifty. And something just isn't right.

It's hard to say exactly what.

It's like there's a shadow in her eyes.

I first noticed it over Christmas. Everything was perfect, of course, as it is every year. The family gathered at our place in Sydney, including our three grown kids and their families, Pam's very elderly dad and brother, my folks and my sister Louise with her four kids. They come to us because it's what they've always done. Pam wouldn't dream of having it any other way.

They all pitched in, in their own way. Pam and our two girls spent Christmas morning in the kitchen preparing vegies for roasting. Pam's dad paid for the turkey. Her brother brought the bonbons, and Louise made her usual, the world's second-best fruit pudding, runner-up to the one Pam makes me every May for my birthday.

We sat down for the traditional turkey roast for lunch, with all the trimmings. The food was fantastic. The chatter was cheery. I sat at the head of the table, with Pam to my left. I relaxed into that special comfort that comes from conforming to customs. When Pam sat down after serving the coffee, I reached out from my peaceful haven of habit and squeezed her hand in a silent secret celebration of making it through another Christmas lunch together.

I always wink. She always smiles. But this year, the shadow was there, stopping the smile from reaching her eyes. She broke the glance too quickly and dove into conversation with her brother on her left, missing my concerned but silent enquiry.

After lunch, it was the men's turn in the kitchen, loading the dishwasher, washing those that didn't fit, and stowing leftovers in the Bethlehem fridge, with no room left in it.

When we finally emerged, I followed the sound of laughter into the back living room and found children in a mangled mess playing Twister, with mums and aunties spurring them on from the couch. But no Pam.

I left the shouts of 'No, your right foot,' behind and went in search of my beloved. I found her at last, in the laundry.

'Surely that could wait until tomorrow, love.'

'I just thought I'd make a start. Not much into Twister.' Pam didn't stop fiddling with the dirty clothes.

'It's fun to watch. How about I get them organised for charades.'

'If you like,' she said quietly. No light in her eyes, no spark in her voice.

I moved closer, took the washing she clung to and threw it to the floor, and placed her empty hands on my hips. Moving closer still, I pulled her into my arms, nuzzling her neck and whispering, 'Let's start the miming with this one.'

I ran my hands gently up and down her spine, lingering over the curvy places, and nibbling on her tasty earlobes. Finally, I felt her relax against my chest.

'Is it a movie or a song title?' she looked at me at last.

'It's whatever you want to make it, my love. It's a promise, an admission, a vow.' My fingers got lost in her silky hair as I cradled her head in my hands.

'I'll write it in poetry or prose.' I ran my thumbs across her cheek.

'I'll sing it.' I caressed her lips with trembling fingers until they formed a fragile smile.

'I'll get my phone and video myself singing it. Then you can watch it on YouTube over and over and over again.'

I leant forward and gently touched my lips to hers.

'Please don't,' she giggled. 'I've heard you sing.'

Her giggle was music to my ears.

'Just so long as you know,' I kissed her again, 'that I'll say it any way I need to so as you know for absolute certain,' my lips just couldn't stay away, 'that I love you.'

I deepened the kiss. Boy, did I love this woman. She could awaken desire in me, even after all these years of being with her. Her response fed the flame of my passion and I was seriously ready to ditch the Christmas guests and take her to our room.

I pulled away for a moment and looked into her eyes. Eyes I knew so well. The light of love had chased the shadow away. Where darkness had lingered there was now fire and sparkle and life.

'There you are,' her dad gave an amused cough. 'I've got them organised for charades. You coming?'

Thus began a week of family fun. The kids always stayed till New Years. We always watched the Boxing Day cricket, even if it was only in the background while the grandchildren explored their

new toys. Leftovers were standard fare. When they ran out, we
started on the ham leg, with all the usual summer salads.

We didn't have to think about how to spend our days. Our
memories imposed the schedule, requiring a bike ride on the 27th, a
beach volleyball tournament on the 28th, and so on through the
week, until the big barbeque bash on New Year's Eve.

Pam participated in the crazy program for the week. She was
there, but something seemed different, as though she wore
sunglasses on the inside of her eyes, keeping her inner light from
getting out.

On New Year's Day, everyone returned to their own homes and
lives. Routine and busyness took over ours, and the coming weeks
fell into a predictable pattern. I learned to live with the shadow. For
all my talking and loving and teasing, I couldn't seem to catch it.
Couldn't chase it away.

One Friday evening late in January, we headed for our favourite
swimming beach after work. Pam had taken ages to get ready, and I
assumed her swimsuit hid beneath the lightweight tracksuit. Grey,
like her countenance. As soon as my toes hit the warm, golden
sand, I dumped my towel and stripped down to my shorts, ready to
grab her hand and run for the ocean.

She was sitting on her carefully laid out towel. In her grey
tracksuit. Staring blankly at the horizon.

'Coming in?'

'Not just yet. You go ahead.'

I splashed in the foam for a bit, but it was no fun without
anyone to dunk. I watched Pam, hoping she was ready to come in.
She sat, unmoving. Unsmiling. Her eyes not focussed, but full of
tears.

I'd caught her crying before. Tried throughout the month to hold her, comfort her. Tried asking what was wrong. Tried tickling it out of her, kissing it out of her. Tried joking her out of her funk. Tried waiting for the right time. Nothing worked.

My attempts were met with 'nothing's wrong,' or 'I don't know.'

If she didn't know, what hope did I have of understanding. I wanted to be patient. I wanted to be loving. I wanted my vibrant, fun-loving wife back.

Rather than get in trouble for nagging her when she cried, again, I swam out my frustration, turning my helplessness into relentless drive, forcing my muscles out of their comfort zone. When they refused to be pushed any further, I headed for the shore, half expecting Pam to have walked home by now.

But, no. She sat facing east, peering out to sea with Norfolk Island pines lining the coast behind her, blocking the beauty of the glorious sunset sky in the west. Like a rogue wave surprising an unsuspecting swimmer, a revelation struck me. To make a shadow, something has to block the light. The light is still there. There's no shadow without the light. Pam still had plenty of life and light in her, I just had to move the trees out of the way.

I hoped they are saplings, not the majestic giants looming over Pam now, immovable.

On Monday I started my detective work. I dropped in on our family doctor during my lunch break and insisted on seeing her.

'You know I couldn't tell you, even if there was something wrong, Brian. Confidentiality. Client privilege. All that.'

'So, you're saying there is something wrong and you're just not telling me.' I started pacing the office, berating myself for not thinking of health issues sooner.

'No. I'm saying that I can't say. I haven't seen Pam in ages. If you're concerned, get her to come in and see me.'

'Yeah. Thanks, Doc. I'll do that.' I didn't think Pam would co-operate, but anything was worth a try.

On my way home from work that night, I stopped by Joe and Maura's place. Pam and Maura had had their first babies together and had been friends ever since. They shared the joy and struggles of first-time motherhood, and tackled every other phase of life by drawing strength from each other. Joe and I tagged along at first, then developed our own friendship. We went fishing together, and to the gym. Our families holidayed together as the kids grew. If anyone knew what was going on with Pam, Maura would.

'I know what you mean, Brian. I've noticed it too. She's just not herself.'

'Have you talked to her about it? The way you girls share everything over the years frightens me sometimes.'

'You really need to talk to her yourself.'

'Not another one of these female conspiracies.' I raked my hands through my hair and tried to keep the rising frustration out of my voice. 'You mean you know something, but you won't betray a confidence.' I lost my battle with anger and found myself yelling, 'What is it with you women?'

'Brian. I don't know anything. I've tried talking to her and she just shrugs and says she doesn't know.'

'Okay…Sorry Maura. It's just that I feel like I'm losing her.'

'She loves you, Brian. Always has. Maybe it's some weird 'she's-not-getting-any-younger' thing.'

'You're about the same age – are you feeling…sad? Or disconnected? Do you cry a lot?'

'Well, no,' Maura threw her hands in the air and walked away, pausing thoughtfully. 'Not all women are the same, you know. I'm too busy to feel disconnected. It's all I can do to keep up with the grandkids who've taken over their parent's bedrooms to finish high school in the city.'

I headed for home, feeling discouraged, but determined. Then discouraged all over again when Pam refused to see the doctor. She assured me she was perfectly well, and that everything was fine at her last check-up.

When I went to change out of my work clothes, Pam called after me, 'Have you made the booking for Valentine's Day? It's only two weeks away. I'll do it if you're too busy.'

Curious, I walked back to where she stood, hoping to see a glow of excited anticipation. Instead, I saw the same glum indifference I'd grown accustomed to seeing, along with the slumped shoulders. And, of course, the ever-present shadow.

For our entire married life, we'd made a ritual out of dressing up, catching a train across town, and dining at the French restaurant on Main Street. We didn't go there any other time. We prioritised the evening to keep the romance in our marriage, getting babysitters when the kids were younger. The year they all had the flu, we drove, and skipped dessert to make it quicker, but we still went.

I thought we both enjoyed it. I loved the stability of it, year in and year out. It was romantic. It was special, to me. And I'd

229

assumed to Pam too. But watching her without her knowing, seeing her cool disinterest, was like having a bucket of cold water thrown over me.

With the water came revelation and I backed away, sinking onto our bed in astonishment. It wasn't stable; it was boring. I wasn't being romantic; I was being lazy. There was nothing special about going to the same place every year. A light began to dawn.

'Did you hear me?' Pam came into the room, looking for an answer. I wondered if I'd finally found mine.

'No, don't worry. I'll handle the Valentine's Day arrangements,' I assured her.

* * * * *

On February 13th, I sat Pam down after work.

'We're doing Valentine's Day a little differently this year.'

'Oh.' Was that a spark of interest I detected?

'Yes. It's a surprise, but you'll need to be ready at noon, with an overnight bag packed for both of us. I have to work in the morning, but I'll pick you up at midday.'

My plan seemed to be working before it even began. The smile, the interest, the flirtatious curiosity that oozed from Pam's every pore was worth the hurried arrangements I'd had to make. She badgered me with questions: Where are we going, how long will we be gone, what should she pack? I gave nothing away.

My gorgeous wife looked young and full of life when I got home at noon the next day. I whisked the bags into the car, opened the door for Pam, and refused to answer her questions. She squealed with delight when I took the airport road.

'We're going to Perth?' She nearly knocked me flying with the enthusiasm of her hug when we stopped at the departure gate heading west. 'I can't believe it.'

'I thought we'd try something new. Happy Valentine's Day, darling.' I kissed her broad smile, astounded by the fervency of her response. We lingered there, oblivious to the stares of the crowd.

Going to Perth together was something of a bucket-list item for us. I'd been on business a few times, robbed of Pam's company by demands for her presence at home with the kids. Now she was like a little girl, eager to explore Wonderland as soon as we'd checked into the hotel.

We stayed a week, dining out, sleeping late, indulging in one another like honeymooners. No sign of shadow or sadness, just a blaze of passion, a glow of delight, a vibrant hunger for discovery.

On Friday evening, we headed for a swimming beach recommended by the concierge. Pam had taken ages to get ready, and I assumed her swimmers once again hid beneath the lightweight tracksuit. A fluorescent floral design in golds and yellows, like her countenance. As soon as my toes hit the warm, golden sand, I dumped my towel and stripped down to my shorts, ready to grab her hand and run for the ocean.

'Coming in?'

'Sure.' She stripped down to her bathing suit – new, daring, chosen together on yesterday's voyage of adventure into Perth's retail district. We splashed in the foam for a bit, appreciating the warmth of the ocean. I delighted in Pam's playfulness, her ready laughter, her cheeky smile.

'Mmm,' I groaned in pleasure at her kisses. 'You taste just like a peanut. So good salted.'

'I'm heading out now,' she whispered, tugging on my arm, enticing me to join her. 'You coming?'

'Tempting. But I don't want to get arrested for indecent behaviour on a public beach. Think I'll swim for a bit.'

She kissed me again, obviously trying to change my mind.

I resisted, and swam out my pent-up energy, turning my desire into unrelenting drive, forcing my muscles out of their comfort zone. When they refused to be pushed any further, I headed for the shore, half expecting Pam to be asleep on her towel.

But, no. She sat in the reflected glow of an amazing sunset. Norfolk Island pines lining the coast loomed behind her once again, but this time they were to the east, their needles turned a soft shade of pink to match the radiant sky in the west. Like a rogue wave surprising an unsuspecting swimmer, revelation struck me once again.

We'd changed directions. We were on the opposite side of the country. And the trees no longer blocked the flush of the setting sun, leaving it free to bathe in rose gold the exciting woman I was privileged to call my wife.

I sank to my knees in the sand, relief filling me. I had no hope of shifting the trees looming over Pam. Age, hormonal changes, the kids getting busier and busier with their own lives and growing families – these were all immovable, beyond my control. But I could work with Pam to change directions in our lives, find fresh interests to focus on, new projects to empower her.

It was time to update our traditions, to stop doing things a certain way just because we always had. We needed to get creative. Pam didn't need a peaceful haven of habit anymore. She needed the original, the unique.

I looked up and saw her, sitting on her carefully laid-out towel. In her dazzling tracksuit. Staring in awe at the picturesque horizon, the light reflected in her beautiful eyes.

'Hey, I was thinking,' I stretched my towel beside hers, splashing her in the process and delighting in her mock horror. 'Do you think you could make a cheesecake for my birthday this year? I fancy a change from fruit pudding.'

'Growing old is mandatory,
but growing up is optional!'

Walt Disney

Living Off the Land

The land had been Jack's life. He'd worked hard, like all farmers. When the kids had been young, they'd made time as a family for social stuff – sport, community, even church. Then they grew up and left him to it. He had to work harder, and longer. Wasn't long before working the farm was all he had time or energy for.

'So, where're you off to this morning, Love?'

'Fundraising Committee for the CWA. We're planning a huge old-fashioned fete. But I'll be back in time for our walk, and lunch. What are you planning for your day?'

'Well, I guess I might read the paper.'

'Have you thought about a garden, Jack? Vegies cost a fortune here in town, and they're tasteless, insipid things. I'd love to grow our own. It's something we could do together.'

'Not much room to grow anything here. Soil's good though. Maybe it's worth thinking about.'

* * * * *

It took Jack two weeks to think about the vegie garden, and two more to remove the back lawn. He felt good working outside again, except for the closeness, and the noise. Jack couldn't get over how noisy it was in town. He heard the kids down the road playing in their yard. He heard the neighbour sneezing. Not to mention the continual drone of cars on the road. Even natural noises sounded different, like rain pinging off a dozen rooftops and splashing on the bitumen.

Shutting himself inside was the only way to get any peace, but that was unthinkable. He needed fresh air (hoping at a bare minimum for 'not stale, inside air', and only dreaming of 'clean and sweet like country air') from an open window to stop the urban strangulation doing him in. But then, he heard the urban noise. And felt the urban smog sucking the life out of his lungs.

Betty had saved the day last week by suggesting they move their daily walk to the beach now that the weather was improving. Although he'd appreciated her advice about the garden, he wasn't so sure her latest idea had much merit.

'*Humph.*' Jack didn't know what to say to that. Finally, he came up with, 'Aren't we a bit old for that sort of thing.'

'Well, just you give it a try, Old Man. You might find it's exactly what we need.'

How right she'd been. They had to drive before they could walk, but it was worth it. The only sounds were purely natural. The lap of waves, the squawk of seagulls and the whisper of wind through the beach grasses were music to Jack's ears. And the air carried the taste of salt instead of the rancid flavour of exhaust fumes.

Ever since, he'd looked forward to walking along the beach, hand-in-hand with his Betty. Closest he'd been to heaven since leaving the farm.

* * * * *

Betty shuffled to the window in her dressing-gown and slippers, her hair rollers keeping the phone away from her ear. Pulling back the curtain she glanced out.

'Yes, he's out there already,' she said to her friend Joyce. 'I have no idea what he's up to… gotta go… trouble's coming.'

Jack, in his favourite old farm clothes, was bending over, yanking weeds out of his new garden bed. Like a rusty crane unfolding, he straightened up, pushing a dirt-stained fist into the small of his back in an attempt to work out an angry knot in the muscle. He'd been lazy too long and had gone soft. Fancy not even being able to manage a bit of weeding. He'd have to finish it after a good long stretch.

He looked up and groaned when a shadow blocked out the sun, still surrounded by the golden hues of dawn. He saw his neighbour, in an expensive morning coat, strutting across his adjoining yard towards their shared fence.

'Good morning, Jack. You're certainly up with the birds this morning.'

'Mornin',' Jack replied, wishing he could remember the man's name. He always called him 'The Toff' at home. 'Weeds won't wait till after lunch.'

'Nice little garden you have there.'

'Guess so.' Jack wished he'd go back to his fancy house. 'Was that you makin' that racket 'til all hours last night? Kept me and the wife awake with that eternal thump, thump, thump of your music.' Jack kneaded his back harder.

'No, Jack. We had guests last evening, but our dinner party was a quiet, dignified affair. Our friends left by ten.'

'Thought it was comin' from over your way. Would've called the cops if it weren't for the wife beggin' me not to make a fuss.'

'It must have been the folk across from us, Jack. They come and go in that noisy, dirty jalopy of theirs. The street was full of such vehicles last night. It appeared they might have been having a barbeque.'

Everyone seemed to know everybody's doings here in the town.

'*Humph.*' He'd been hiding behind that 'humph' all his life. He supposed it made people think he was a grumpy old man.

'I'm surprised to see you out so early, since you had a disturbed night?'

'Like I said before, the weeds won't wait.' Jack had been up with the sun every day, even when the babies had bawled half the night, or he'd lain awake waiting for teenagers to get in. The land still needed him, almost as much as he needed it.

Stuck in town like this, on their tiny house block, surrounded by Toffs and loud music, Jack was especially grateful for Betty's good ideas, and her persistent nagging. Now that he'd made a start, she wasn't about to let him get out of growing their own vegies.

'Well, Jack, I hope you reap a bountiful harvest after all your hard work. Perhaps I'll go and have a word with last night's wild partiers. I'll see you another time.' He wandered away, whistling.

'Yeah, maybe,' Jack managed, not wanting to overuse the 'humph'. When the Toff was out of earshot, he added, not quite under his breath, 'Not if I see you first.'

He turned and bent again into the garden, pleased to have his hands back in the soil. Pleased that the weeds wouldn't wait, and feeling a sense of mischief returning to his town-wearied soul.

* * * * *

Later in the day, Jack sat at the kitchen table, slurping tea, dunking a large home-baked biscuit. Betty was doing a crossword in the newspaper.

'What did he want?'

'Who? The Toff, ya mean. Tried telling me all that racket was from Joyce and Stan's place last night.'

'Didya tell 'im we were at Joyce and Stan's last night, and there was no loud music?'

'Didn't waste me breath. He was too busy looking down 'is toffy nose at 'em for driving utes from off the farm and 'aving a 'bar-bee-que'.'

Jack downed the last of his tea and eased himself up, leaning heavily on the table.

'You're not heading back out, are you? Don't overdo it, Jack. There's no big rush.'

'Just pulling a few weeds, Love. Nothing like the back-aching work I did on the farm.'

Like an old tractor moving through mud, Jack trudged out. When Betty started humming, he muttered to himself, 'Gotta keep at it if my plan is gonna work.'

* * * * *

Early the following morning, Betty once again shuffled to the window in her dressing-gown and slippers. And once again, she pulled back the curtain in order to better discuss the goings-on with her friend, Joyce, on the phone.

'Yes, Joyce, he's out there again...I'm sure he's up to something...gotta go...there's a truck pulling in.'

Outside, Jack waved his arms excitedly, directing the reversing vehicle to a stop. Before Stan even managed to unfold himself from the cabin, Jack grabbed a shovel, thrusting it into the dark, muddy mound in the back. He smiled as he lofted fresh manure over his garden.

'Didya have any trouble getting this stuff, Stan?'

'No. When I told my son about The Toff, he was pleased as punch to help out.'

'Perfect day for it, hey. That good strong westerly will do the trick just fine.'

Betty ambled down the path.

'Watch out, Jack, you're spraying that stuff everywhere. The rest of the neighbourhood doesn't want to smell it.'

'No harm in good healthy farm smells. Beats town smog any day.'

Jack winked cheekily at Stan, a huge grin on his face.

* * * * *

Jack had weeded and watered and wandered up and down the rows for days inhaling the soothing rural aromas still wafting from his well-fertilized garden, yet anxious to catch the first sign of actual vegies growing. That sense of Christmas-like anticipation, and the fact that he hadn't seen The Toff since his little bit of foolery, had him feeling like a kid again, except for more than the odd ache. He felt good, and much more like his old self for the first time since they'd sold the farm.

Stooping low, he checked out a green shoot – it looked like a tiny tomato plant. Definitely not a weed.

'Yes!' Jack smiled. 'I've still got it. I can coax life, even from this urban soil.'

He might just manage living off the land after all.

'Old age, believe me, is a good and pleasant thing.
It is true you are gently shouldered off the stage,
but then you are given
such a comfortable front stall as spectator.'

Confucius

Unprecedented

Sylvia huffed as she picked up the weighty shopping bags once again and staggered up the remaining steps to her front door. She would have liked to buy more groceries, but that would have involved a longer stay at the supermarket, and she just couldn't risk it.

She fumbled in her pocket for her keys, scanning the street, desperate to get in before anybody came. Gasping for breath which she seemed to have been holding forever, she slammed the door, leaning against it, exhausted but safe.

She'd made it.

The events of the last few days flooded her mind. Her world had gotten smaller incrementally, in inverse proportion to the media's crisis vocabulary. It seemed to expand hourly to include barely used words like pandemic, lockdown, COVID-19, self-isolation and epicentre – wasn't that something to do with earthquakes? As they told her repeatedly, the situation and everything about it was unprecedented.

Sylvia thought she and Ron had faced their fair share of fresh challenges. It came with the territory for their generation, who'd grown up in a world recovering from a World War. But this, apparently, was something else, something worse than thalidomide, terrorism, nuclear arms or AIDS. Something unprecedented.

And she was facing it without Ron.

She craved the latest news, gulping in Corona stats like a diver taking in air after staying down too long. She had to know where things were at, how bad it was.

But she'd be okay. She'd survived the anniversary of Ron's death, and the first Christmas without him. Once again she deliberately slowed her breathing and repeated her oft-used mantra: She'd be okay. Only this time she added something new: She'd stay home and she'd be okay.

She had no reason to go out anyway. Her spinning group had cancelled their meetings, Bingo was abandoned until further notice and her pantry was always well stocked. Her frantically brief outing today had provided more essentials, and she started to believe she would be okay.

Mostly.

Sylvia's days fell into a routine. She soon delighted in the sameness of them, the predictability. Her day started with an early phone call from one of her family, unnecessarily stressing the importance of routine and self-care. She wondered if they had a roster. They were trying to teach her how to do 'Facetime' (whatever that was), but technology had never really been her thing. The rest of the day proceeded blissfully with very few interruptions until she exercised on her patio at lunchtime.

After an afternoon of game shows and soap operas, Sylvia cooked up a storm. No more processed easy-meals for her. The TV news was on, but while they droned on about flattening the curve, Sylvia discovered new and delightful ways to enhance hers. Imagine if she wasn't exercising! Instead of inhaling COVID stats, Sylvia sniffed the spicy aromas of cuisine from around the world.

Friends phoned occasionally, complaining about the restrictions. Sylvia tried to sound sympathetic, but she was unexpectedly enjoying her small world. Instead of going ballroom dancing every Monday fortnight, because Mavis said the class needed more females, Sylvia found renewed joy in reading. Rather than providing Harriet with accountability at the gym in her retirement complex on Tuesdays and Thursdays, Sylvia discovered she was rather good at writing poetry, and loved it.

Wednesday afternoons used to involve volunteering at an old folk's home, calling Bingo numbers, serving cake, talking loudly. Now she corresponded with pen and paper, wishing the elderly residents well in their isolation, glad she wasn't ready for that lifestyle permanently just yet.

She wasn't just okay – she was excellent, content, happy.

Breathing in the wondrous scent of homemade hot cinnamon donuts, Sylvia realised her out-every-other-night-lifestyle was all about keeping other people happy, and proving she could manage without Ron. Yet, she was perfectly content staying home, sorting cupboards, doing jigsaw puzzles, teaching herself to find games on her computer, and watching old movies. And, just occasionally, eventually, reaching out to others via Facetime.

Later, when she could, she enjoyed going for long, slow walks in the freshness of her brand-new world, noticing things she'd seen before, but not acknowledged because she was distracted by the ever-present demands of her schedule: the sounds the birds made in the early mornings; the smell of leaves dampened by overnight rain; the laughter of children in a nearby park.

She didn't want to return to a life that excluded such beauty. She'd discovered something wonderful in lockdown. Something she wished she'd worked out decades earlier. Something freeing: she was an introvert.

She'd heard the term on one of the morning shows on TV, on one of the days she broke her self-imposed no-television-before-lunch rule. And again on some talk-back psychology program on late-night radio. Once she'd heard it, it seemed to crop up everywhere. It seemed being an introvert and 'owning it' was not just acceptable – it was trendy.

Along with her shaky efforts at Facetime, it proved the old adage about never being too old to learn something new. Here she was, thinking she'd lived her life and survived quite well being shy, but she realised now, it was only because Ron's friendliness balanced her. His extroversion had drawn her out, helped her manage in social situations. All along, she'd been more than shy – she'd been an introvert. It explained a lot about her past.

And yet, she could tell that her growing awareness of the term, its meaning, and how it so accurately defined and explained her would also impact her future. Even without Ron to help, her fresh understanding gave her the courage to invite the unprecedented into her own life by being true to herself.

She'd start saying 'no' more often. Not to everything, but just enough to ensure there was time to be herself. It would take some getting used to, but she'd survived, even thrived through the pandemic, and she knew one thing for certain – she'd be okay.

'Do not grow old, no matter how long you live.
Never cease to stand like curious children before the great mystery
into which we were born.'

Albert Einstein

I Was There

'Gammar, can you be my show 'n tell at school tomorrow?' The back door clattered shut behind seven-year-old John as he hurried to find his great-grandmother. Betsy startled, embarrassed at being caught dozing in the rocking chair her daughter had put on the back veranda for that very purpose.

'Why would anyone at school be interested in what this ol' lady has to say, John?'

'Well, we been learning about our beginnings in this country, Gammar, and the teacher tells it different to what I've heard from you.'

'How can that be, John? What's your teacher saying?'

'Well, he ain't said nothing 'bout the surprises.'

'Well, it's not much of a story without them, now is it?'

'Tell me the story again, Gammar. Tell me again about the surprises waiting here for you that first day.'

'Well,' she couldn't resist the pleading in his eyes, 'I woke up that first morning on the beach of Port Jackson. It took me a while to work out where I was. Wakefulness seeped through my brain, gently chasing my dreams away like sunrise dispersing shadows.

249

The first thing I noticed was the stillness. I was no longer being rocked by ocean waves.'

John settled into a chair beside her.

'I'd spent nearly nine months aboard the *Lady Penrhyn*, tossed on the high seas, surrounded by sea-sickness, home-sickness and soul-sickness. Finally, I'd spent a night on solid ground.'

'But you hadn't slept before then, Gammar. Don't forget the part about the gaol.'

'You're right, John, I hadn't slept well even before I sailed halfway around the world. It started when I chanced to steal some cheese from a market stall. It was the only way I could think to feed my hungry younger brothers and sisters. But luck was not on my side. I got caught and landed meself in Newgate Prison, along with half of London, it seemed. I spent weeks trying to sleep there, three to a bunk, not trusting the women around me enough to close both eyes.

'I made one friend there, though. Lizzie. She knew how to handle the rough girls. Chance was on my side this time and Lizzie and me managed to stay together when some toff in an office somewhere got it into his head to make some changes. He set to fixing the overcrowding in London's gaols by moving prisoners into old ships in the Thames River. The authorities called those dark, damp, disease-ridden, rotting ships 'hulks'. I called them home for untold months. We lived surrounded by floggings, hard labour, hopelessness and death. And a stench I've never forgot.

'But, back to that first day... the memory of that foul odour paled as I realised everything had changed, again. The freshness in the air wasn't a dream. It lingered even after I was fully awake. The air was scented with pure crispness, the sun was bright, even at that early hour, and I wished I could soak in the novelty of it forever.'

'But it gets so hot in the sun, Gammar.'

'Yes, but it was so different from England's dullness. Even the summers back there seemed gloomy compared to the brightness we found here.

'We wanted to explore a bit before the guards came and assigned us to work details. Even remembering I was a convict, bound to obey commands for nearly seven more years, seemed less offensive in this fresh, bright place, with these women.'

'Teacher said they was awful, nasty women, Gammar?'

'He might think that, but a strange comradery had developed, replacing the catfighting and distrust. We'd shared such horrific conditions for so long. And we all felt the terror of starting over in a strange new land. It bonded us together. Adversity united us as we spent night after storm-tossed night wondering aloud and worrying about what we faced halfway around the earth.

'Lizzie and I were just folding up our rough, scratchy blankets when raucous laughter erupted from a stand of nearby trees.'

'Ah, I love the kookaburra part.' John mimicked the maniacal titter of his favourite bird.

'Well, I didn't know it was a kookaburra when I heard it that day. I didn't know what it was. Lizzie and I inched gingerly toward the unfamiliar trees. The cackling turned hysterical and we couldn't help but laugh along, especially when we discovered it was a bird laughing at us.

'We hadn't had a good laugh in such a long time. We decided this new land could well be full of surprises. And not all bad ones at that. We wandered further, marvelling at the glorious gum trees, different from anything we'd ever seen before. The bright red waratah, and the pink and red bottlebrushes surprised us with their bold beauty. So much vivid colour, hidden amongst the grey-green bush.'

'What about the guards, Gammar? Teacher said they were mean and brutal to you convicts.'

'He's right, at least in the beginning. The marines charged with guarding us on board were as cruel and callous as the prison guards, or worse, ready to thrash a trouble-maker with their cat o' nine tails. Then, as we sailed further from home, they changed. They were tossed on wild seas for endless months just like we were. They too suffered the lousy food, the lack of water and hygiene, and the fear of the unknown. And it tempered some of them.

'They never admitted to being afraid, of course, or softened enough to show a moment's kindness. They had an image to protect, after all. But chances are, deep down, they were as homesick and as terrified as I was over having to live so far from everything we knew.'

'You didn't know the animals either, did you Gammar?'

'We brought some familiar ones with us – like the horses that sailed on the *Lady Penrhyn* with me. But just imagine how it felt to see the unique animals of this new land peeking out from their hiding places to welcome us: the kangaroo, bounding about using its tail like a third leg; the koala, balancing in the fork of a tree with a baby on its back; and the emu. What were we to make of that strange new creature? We'd never seen anything like those peculiar animals before. More and more wondrous surprises in this place.'

'There's one other thing Teacher said, Gammar. You have to come and set him straight. He told us the natives were primitive and hostile.'

'Sadly, John, people try to make heroes of themselves by making others look bad. When we first came across the people who lived here long before we arrived, they were as curious about us as we were about them. But timid and suspicious too, just like us. Sometimes we amused them, like when the men tried to cut down the enormously strong trees to build with, and their tools broke. It wasn't so funny when they blasted those trees right out of the ground with gunpowder. A frightening noise for such quiet, gentle people.

'Our arrival meant as much change for them as we were facing, but I discovered that, like anyone, if we treated them respectfully, they were civil back, helpful even. As far as surviving here goes, they were way smarter than us. Don't know how we would've made it without their help.'

John jumped up from his chair. 'Now, Gammar, tell me again about the best surprise of all.'

'You mean apart from the joy of the kookaburra, the boldness of the waratah, the uniqueness of the bush animals, and the kindness of the native people.' Betsy was teasing her great-grandson, knowing full well he knew the story by heart. He wiggled and squirmed, eagerly anticipating the words he loved.

'Come on, Gammar.'

'Well, you know it wasn't all easy. Things were tough. It was hard getting used to different weather, unusual animals, unpredictable people.'

'How'd you do it, Gammar? What made you keep going?' John was nearly beside himself with expectation.

'I'd felt hopeless for so long, ever since my dad was killed in the mines back in England, leaving me, the oldest, to provide for six siblings and ma, who never quite recovered from her grief. Things only got worse when I stole to feed my family, and in gaol, despair set in. Now, here I was in this brand-new land, full of its unique and special treasures, hidden here just for me to discover, right when I needed them most.

'It was like the biggest treasure hunt ever, and each time I found a treasure, I felt unique and special too. The more I discovered, the stronger the feeling got. I felt hope rising up inside me for the first time in forever. It was exactly what I needed to start my new life in this new land with all its challenges.'

'That's what Teacher needs to hear, Gammar. Bert could do with knowing it too, since his Dad broked his leg so he has to do all the work. And what about all the farmers needing rain? Hope'd help them too. Why doesn't Teacher tell it your way?'

'Well, yes, they need hope more than anyone, but your teacher only knows what he's heard, and read. I know how it was that first day, because I was there.'

'Will you come and tell it your way, Gammar.'

'I'd love to, John.'

With age comes... wisdom

Most dictionaries define wisdom along the lines of
having the experience and knowledge required to make sensible
decisions or give good advice.
They suggest synonyms like discernment, insight, good sense,
experience, knowledge, and good judgement.
I'd suggest another synonym – maturity or older age.

People who have lived for as long as older people have lived
just can't help but have experience – whether they were
successful at everything they turned their hand to
or look back over their lives with regret – they experienced it,
and thus, by definition, they are able to give good advice.

And even if they never finished school all those years ago,
they've acquired knowledge just by surviving all those years,
which again qualifies them to give good advice.

But, advice is only any good if you heed it,
which starts with listening.

We need to treat older people and their advice with dignity,
because their wisdom has been hard-earned through trial and error,
good times and bad.
That's how it works with experiencing life.

So listen to every memory, every crazy story. A hidden gem
of wisdom might just jump out and surprise you.

Unseen Wonder

Julia strolled through the house one last time. Her home. The centre of her world for so long. The bedroom, where she'd slept beside the same man for forty-four years. And picked up his yesterday's socks every morning, as though the laundry hamper moved.

In their bathroom, she inhaled the sensuous scent of his aftershave. After all these years, it still gave her goosebumps, bombarding her mind with memories of the passion they shared. Dan was one fine-smelling man. Her man. She stood, hugging his towel to her face, as if inhaling more of him would change things.

Moving on, she peeped into Micah's old room. His sanctuary. He was the last of their kids to leave the nest, nearly a year ago now, and she just hadn't had the heart to remove all trace of him and turn it into yet another spare room. So his Jeffrey Archer collection remained on the bookshelf he'd made with a lot of help from his dad. And the bottom drawer still overflowed with charging cords for appliances he'd thrown away years ago. Today, though, Julia simply smiled and walked away. None of it really mattered much. He was a fine boy. Well, more like a fine man, actually.

Julia straightened the towels in the main bathroom, pushed the coffee table back into position in the TV room, and carried Dan's breakfast dishes to the sink. Her resolve was still strong. She would leave all this.

Today.

The thought of going had been nagging her for a while. No one needed her here anymore. She wasn't running away from anything horrible, she was running toward the something more she knew there had to be. She couldn't find it here. She'd looked for too long already.

She'd packed yesterday, after searching for her grandmother's old suitcase in the attic. She placed a carefully worded note on the table with her keys, pulled the door behind her, and walked away.

Julia's train took several hours to get to Sydney, where she could hide more easily. Dan would think she'd gone north to her sister's. He'd never look for her in Sydney, and she'd have time alone to find whatever it was she was searching for.

The repetitious rumble of the train seemed at one minute to chant, *'Go home. Go home. Go home,'* and the next it was rattling out an excited, *'You're free. You're free. You're free.'* Julia knew just how it felt.

Confused.

Arriving in Sydney, Julia collected her suitcase and drew herself up with pride. She was a competent, capable woman. She was also a hungry, thirsty woman. Her first independent decision was to find a café and get something to eat and drink. For too many years she had put the needs of everyone else ahead of her own, but this time she was free to do what she wanted, when she wanted. It felt strange.

It felt good.

Across the road, Julia spotted a quaint little café. The lights were on, but the door was closed. As she approached, she saw an 'OPEN. PLEASE ENTER' sign and pushed through the door.

Her senses were immediately captivated by the place. It was warm, with cosy tables and comfy chairs, all decorated in soft, autumnal shades. But what struck her most was the fragrance. The air was permeated with apple and cinnamon. And perhaps a hint of nutmeg.

Julia was instantly carried back to her grandmother's kitchen. Oh, the hours she'd spent there as a girl! Nan let her crack the eggs, mix the batter and, best of all, lick the spoon.

Julia emerged from her reverie long enough to take a seat and order, then quickly returned to Nan's kitchen, where she drank the special milky tea laced with honey that she only ever had at Nan's place. They'd sit at the table and natter like old ladies, between bites of the apple crumble muffins they'd just made together. During school holidays, Julia stayed longer with Nan, and learnt how to knit and sew and make patchwork.

Julia was so far down memory lane she didn't notice she had company until the elderly lady sitting opposite cleared her throat.

'I hope you don't mind. You have such a contented look on your face, I wanted to meet you.'

Julia's dazed look and silence encouraged the woman to continue.

'I'm Mae Franklin, the owner of this establishment.'

'You have an amazing place here, Mrs Franklin. I have one question for you, though.'

'I'm sorry dear, we don't give out recipes. Family secret, you know.'

'No. No. I was wondering why you keep the door closed. This place smells so incredible. And the city smells so dirty. You'd attract heaps more customers if you opened up the doors and windows and let the fragrance out.'

'Well, I'll tell you, dear. We used to do just that. But we found that the odour of the city seeped in and ruined the air in here way before our scent permeated the smog out there. I think it's the same with life, you know.'

'In what way, Mrs Franklin?'

'Oh well. The busyness and humdrum of everyday life so often drowns out the spectacular that happens every day. We get so bogged down with the ordinary, we don't see or smell or feel the extraordinary. Then we turn around and say life's boring, when it is actually full of wondrous things.'

Her wrinkled hand squeezed Julia's as Mae rose to leave. Julia recognised the wisdom in her words.

'I know you can't see it now, dear, but there is much to marvel at around you. There's wonder in the city. There's even wonder in your life. Take a good look, dear. See the wonder.'

* * * * *

For the week that followed, Julia stayed in a hotel and began every day breakfasting with Mae. She found herself pouring out her thoughts to the woman with the cinnamon perfume. She was nearly as good a listener as Nan had been, absorbing every word like it was the most important thing she could be doing at the time, making Julia feel cherished. Special.

Not that Mae held her tongue entirely.

'You make Dan sound so delightful, I feel I should chastise you for leaving the dear man in the lurch. I'm sure he's worried about you.'

This provoked Julia to send a brief 'Don't worry, I'm okay,' text. She ignored the backlog of texts and switched her phone off quickly – she wasn't ready to hear from Dan, or anyone, just yet.

After breakfast, Julia strolled Sydney's streets, looking in shop windows, checking out historical sites, doing whatever she felt like doing. She noticed little bits of wonder everywhere: the cutest little girl, dressed all in pink, scurrying to keep up with the long strides her father took; the bravery of the pioneers depicted in the museum displays; the heavenly aromas somehow seeping from the food shops she passed.

As she adjusted to being alone, and was more confident, she explored further afield, conquering the public transport system, and especially delighting in riding the ferry. The contrasts in this great city amazed her, from skyscrapers to sandy beaches, crowded streets to finely manicured gardens, and everything in between.

She ate lunch in various parks overlooking the harbour. In the beauty of the white-tipped waves, the blue of the sky, the myriad of colours in the flowers around her, she found more of Mae's wonder. It was there in the strength of the Harbor Bridge, the majesty of the Opera House, the variety of architecture throughout the city.

But not everything she noticed that week was altogether wonderful: a sad-looking girl on a nearby bench, trying to blend into her surroundings; a tattered-looking man asleep in the rotunda; a worn-out mum struggling to push a rickety stroller and drag two toddlers up the slope. Was there anything amazing or marvellous in their lives?

On her way back to the hotel, she took more notice of the people around her. The busy businesspeople somehow managed to text without walking into anybody or anything. Stressed people rushed to and fro. Young people with earbuds in, who walked in packs, but were really alone. Were they awestruck by anything in their lives?

She found nothing spectacularly breath-taking when she flicked the television on in her room each evening. Definitely not in the news or the current affairs shows. No wonder the world was in such a mess.

One evening, she wanted to wash off the city's grime. A bubble bath would do the job nicely. She could soak in the suds while Mae's wisdom soaked into her soul.

She found bubbles, set the taps just right and turned to her suitcase for fresh clothes. If she'd realised she would still be here after a week, she may have unpacked. As she opened the suitcase, the smell of mothballs overwhelmed Julia, accompanied by more memories of Nan. The smell had gone unnoticed at home, perhaps proving Mae right, again. Julia had been so focussed on her boredom with the ordinary she had missed both the smell and the wondrous memories it evoked.

She took her thoughts with her to the bathroom and immersed herself fully in the warm bubbles and the good times with Nan.

She sat up with a start as she remembered her childhood. As a wave of suds spilled over the side of the bath, she realised that all she'd ever wanted as a child was a life like Nan's. She'd wanted a husband to love and a home to keep. She'd wanted children who would grow up feeling special and good about themselves because she was their mother. She'd wanted to bake cakes for their lunches, sew buttons on their shirts, and cook all their favourite meals. She wanted to be needed and important to others, just like Nan was to her.

The truth was as chilling as the cooling bath water. She'd had all that and should've been grateful she hadn't needed to work outside the home. Instead, she'd ended up bored. How had Nan remained so full of life and joy despite the drudgery of her domestic life? Several hot water top-ups later, the answer came to her through more delightful memories – of Nan packing a picnic for them to enjoy in the park one gorgeous spring day; of helping Nan decorate a cake with swirls and sweets and dollops of cream, then giving it away to a family in need; of Nan embroidering flowers on hand-me-down clothes so Julia wouldn't feel sad about being in her sister's cast-offs. Nan filled even the most everyday moment with delight. And made Julia, and everyone else she met, feel special.

Julia's confusion and despair drained away as the water drained out of the bath. She emerged with new resolve.

She wasn't sure how, but she knew she needed to follow Nan's example, and heed Mae Franklin's advice. She'd found plenty to marvel at around the city. Now she needed to look within, and find the wonder in her own life.

Drifting off to sleep later that night, Julia dreamed of walking through her home again, just like on the morning she left. Things looked so different. She saw the flowers on her dressing table, a gift from Dan, for no special reason. She smelt his aftershave and remembered their honeymoon. She saw the unfinished quilt in her sewing room, which she expected to one day complete for a grandchild. The Star Wars poster on Micah's wall brought memories of venturing out at midnight to be the first to see it with him.

She woke in the wee hours, her mind still whirring with the wonder that filled her life.

Despite the crazy hour, she had to ring Dan.

She assured him she was fine, and he was so loving, so completely understanding. So wonderful.

'Just come home,' he repeated like a chiming clock, set on the quarter hour. 'I'll do anything I can to make it right.'

Then he listened while she tried to explain.

He said he needed her, not to keep the house and iron the shirts, 'Because you complete me, Julia. Without you, I'm not whole. You know my thoughts; you finish my sentences. You fill in the gaps I leave out.'

How could she argue with that?

'Come home and let me rediscover the wonder in our lives with you. Better yet, tell me where you are and I'll come to you. We can have a second honeymoon in Sydney. What would you like to do?'

'I'd love to introduce you to someone.'

'Who?'

'Mae Franklin. The lady who taught me to hunt down wonder in everyday situations.'

'You mean the lady who reminded you to.'

'Oh, yes, it was Nan who taught me first.'

'And you always wanted to be just like her.'

'How come you're so smart?'

'It all started when I fell in love with you.'

Julia enjoyed the silly, school-crush sort of banter for a while, then fell quiet.

'You sound thoughtful all of a sudden,' Dan was as in-tune with her as he claimed she was with him.

'I've seen so many people here who don't experience any wonder in their lives. I wish there was some way of helping them, of sharing the way it's changed my life.'

'Well, if there's a way, you're the woman to find it.'

Julia couldn't stifle a yawn. 'It makes me tired just thinking of trying.'

'Well, wonderful lady, you get some sleep. I'll be on the first train in the morning.'

'I'll meet you at Mae's for brunch.'

Julia moved across the room. Standing at the window, she saw the first glow of dawn over the harbour. The start of a new chapter in her life. With Dan's confidence in her, and Mae's wisdom, she would surely think of a way of helping sad-looking girls on benches, tattered-looking men sleeping in rotundas or worn-out mums struggling with toddlers to see even the small marvellous things in their lives. The things that make it all worthwhile.

That would make Julia's day wonderful. And her tomorrows too.

'Grandchildren are the crowning glory of the aged;
parents are the pride of their children.'

from the Bible, Proverbs 17:6 (New Living Translation)

Relative Busyness

Chloe totalled the page of entries in her driving log book. Again. She was horrified to find she'd added correctly. That the total hadn't grown since she added it two weeks ago. She threw herself back onto her bed. Frustrated. Helpless.

Her birthday was a month away. She'd be the only eighteen-year-old she knew who wasn't on P-plates. And there was nothing she could do about it. She couldn't go driving without a supervising driver. Everyone in her life who qualified was too busy.

Always too busy.

Dad was pacing and fuming when she rushed into the kitchen the next morning.

'Hurry up, Chloe. Why are you always running late?'

Chloe glanced at the kitchen clock. It was ten minutes before they usually left. No point saying anything. Dad was always right. Or liked to think so.

'If only you'd get your act together and learn to drive, you could take yourself to school instead of making me late every morning. Come on. Let's go.'

Chloe wanted to suggest that, perhaps, he could do more to help. Instead, she grabbed an apple from the fruit bowl, heaved her backpack onto her shoulder and followed Dad out the door. Since Mum wasn't home from her night shift yet, it was Dad or walk.

Chloe realised the ten-minute drive would be the perfect opportunity to explain the seventy-five hours of supervised driving needed before she drove independently. Again. Had he forgotten already or maybe he just wasn't paying attention when she'd told him before. Then her Dad's phone rang and he talked the whole way to school. He never even acknowledged she was leaving.

It was probably just as well. She would only have made him angry.

* * * * *

Mum was having coffee at the kitchen table when Chloe staggered in after school, her back aching from lugging her backpack for the fifteen-minute walk. That would stop once she was driving herself. Maybe Mum had time for some practice.

Then Chloe remembered the last time she drove with Mum. It was two weeks ago and the frenzied yelling still echoed in her ears. Chloe had struggled to focus straight ahead so as not to see her Mum gripping the armrest and pounding the passenger side floor with a foot desperate to find an invisible brake pedal. No wonder the last entry in the log book was only fifteen minutes.

She had a page of entries. After a year on her L's. One page. That page amounted to only four hours. Her friends had stopped listening to her whingeing months ago. It was alright for them. They were the ones driving themselves to school, and to parties, and to after-school jobs. She was the one begging for a ride.

In light of these tragic facts, Chloe ignored the flashback.

'Got time for some driving practice, Mum?'

'Aahh...Well...I don't know, Chloe. It didn't go so well last time.'

An understatement.

'Besides, with Grandpa coming to stay tomorrow, I need to get organised.'

Always too busy.

* * * * *

Grandpa was pottering in the yard when Chloe got home from school the following day.

'How's life with you, Chloe?' He straightened up. 'You shouldn't be walking with that huge weight on your shoulder. Not driving yet?'

'That's a long story, Grandpa.'

'Well, how about you tell me over a cuppa? Better still, how about you drive me to the shopping centre and I'll shout you a milkshake.'

'Are you sure you've got time, Grandpa?'

'I've always got time for important things, Chloe. Like outings with my granddaughter.'

Chloe grabbed her licence and L-plates and hurried to catch up with Grandpa, who was already settling in the passenger seat of his car.

'You've done this before, right? You know how to get started, and where you're going?'

'Sure. There's a checklist I have to go through before I start.'

'You just do whatever you have to. I have complete faith in you.'

Funny thing was, the way he sat back in his seat, looking at the sky and humming softly, made it seem as if he really did believe in her.

A couple of times along the way, Grandpa stopped humming to say, 'Watch out for this guy. He doesn't know where he's going,' or, 'Don't get too close to this one. They're all over the road.'

So, he was paying attention after all.

'Always remember, Chloe, it's the other people on the road you've got to worry about. They're the unpredictable ones, whether they are in a car, on a bike, or on foot. Always look out for the unexpected.'

'Okay, Grandpa, I'll remember that.'

Chloe had taken back streets to the shopping centre, and parked in a side street, not ready to tackle a busy carpark just yet. She hoped Grandpa was too distracted by his rant to notice. She kept him chatting through the outing, and it wasn't until they were back in the car after their milkshakes that Grandpa commented.

'What you need is more confidence, young lady, and that will only come with practice. Give you a few more goes at this trip and you'll be taking the main roads in your stride, and parking in the actual car park.'

So, he had noticed.

'I guess that's why they make us do seventy-five hours with a supervising driver.' Chloe pulled away from the curb and headed home.

'Exactly. How many have you done?'

'Hardly any.'

'I suppose your parents are always too busy to take you driving.' Grandpa was quiet the rest of the way home.

As Chloe nosed into the driveway, he unveiled his scheme. 'How's this for a plan, Kiddo? I'll talk your folks into letting me stay on, at least until your birthday, which I seem to remember is coming up in a month or so. We'll get a big chunk of those hours done together.'

Finally. Someone who wasn't too busy for Chloe.

Though I look old, yet I am strong and lusty;

William Shakespeare
(Adam in *As You Like It*: Act 2, Scene 3)

One-hundred-year-old Feet

I was washing one-hundred-year-old feet. Feet that had been around since World War One ended. Feet that had seen three times as many decades as my own.

As my hands gently rubbed the sudsy loofah over toes that had been washed by a mother born in eighteen hundred and something, my mind imagined how many miles they'd walked, and then how many kilometres. Had they travelled far from home? Had they danced the night away with a soldier, or a farmer? Had they been swollen during pregnancy?

I guessed feet didn't get to be that old without adventures. These feet had surely faced trials and challenges, known pain and hardship, celebrated joys and triumphs. What stories they could tell.

Fortunately, the one-hundred-year-old feet that had piqued my curiosity belonged to a woman with an acutely vibrant mind.

'How long have you been collecting owls?' I asked, remembering my all-too-recent training to look around the house for talking points. Doris had owls everywhere – in pictures on the walls, in china cabinets, embroidered onto every cushion and the quilt on her bed. There were owls on the kitchen clock, to match those on the tea set, naturally.

'Of course I got out the towels.' Doris growled. 'There's two fresh ones on the rail behind you.' I assured her, loudly, that she was right.

That was one thing my aged care course hadn't taught me – perhaps because it was so obvious. People don't wear their hearing aids in the shower! So it's best to keep conversation to the essentials and save the chatty stuff for later.

Doris didn't really need my help, it seemed. It took a while, but she even managed to dry those centenarian feet. Her eyes shone brightly from a face that had clearly endured many an Australian summer. The cheeky twinkle I saw there as she rejected my offer of more help suggested a stubborn independence and a sense of humour that may well have contributed to her longevity.

Washing Doris's feet was the only part of the personal care routine I was allowed to help with that first visit. She'd been managing well enough without help for all but the first few of her one hundred years, so handing over the reins didn't come easily.

Once the hearing aides were in, I was tempted to rush in with questions, my eager curiosity hungry for details. I soon realised that wasn't how it was going to work with Doris. She had a regular morning schedule, and, because she'd been alone since her husband died twenty years ago, chatting wasn't part of it. We talked about the weather, of course. And how her favourite football team was doing, but I carried the majority of the conversation.

I visited Doris three times a week, and after several weeks of washing those one-hundred-year-old feet, I graduated to being allowed to apply moisturiser to them. And delve a little deeper into Doris's story. While the morning cuppa brewed in the owl-adorned teapot, I asked about her family.

'I birthed eight live babies,' she said, a far-away look in her eyes. I thought that might be all I got, until she continued, 'One stillborn. I never even got to hold her. The last one, John, had cerebral palsy.'

'That must have been hard,' I said.

'They didn't expect him to live ten years. He was nearly thirty when he died.'

'You obviously looked after him very well,' I offered lamely, unable to imagine how hard that must have been, especially way back then.

'I fixed up our station wagon with a bed in the back,' she was standing taller now, 'so I could take him with me on weekends to watch the others play football.' She paused thoughtfully. 'It got harder during the polio years,' Doris's shoulders slumped under the weight of remembered grief. 'That awful disease took three of them. But not Johnny.'

'Do any of your family live close by now?' I tried, needing to lighten the moment. It was nearly time for me to go.

'There's only Margaret left now.' Doris paused for so long I didn't think she was going to go on. Then, 'Liz died when she was fifty-five, Michael when he was forty, and Peter was only thirty-eight.'

I reached out and lay my hand on her arm. There was nothing I could say. A mother shouldn't have to bury even one of her children, yet Doris had buried eight. Before she looked away, I saw tears forming in those aged eyes.

'And it was all my fault,' she murmured as she walked to her armchair, the well-steeped tea long forgotten.

'Surely not,' I said quietly, tucking a hand-knitted rug around her legs.

'Some evil quirk in the gene pool, they told me. If I'd married someone else…'

She left the thought unfinished, and I had no time to probe. As it was, I'd be late for my next client.

I handed her the morning paper and tried to distract her with the headline, hoping to leave her in a less melancholy mood.

I kept it light for several visits after that, chatting about the antics of my little dog, and a new shopping centre in the town.

Several weeks later, when I had a bit longer to spend with Doris and the hearing aides were in, I ventured again into meaningful conversation. I pointed to a sepia wedding photo on the bedside drawers, starting with, 'Is that you and your husband?'

'Yes, that's my Frank.'

Again with the short answers. 'He's very handsome.' I offered, then waited, hoping for more information.

'I was only nineteen when I married him. Then he rushed off to war. He was different when he came home.' Doris sat, mesmerised by the photo, and the memories it brought. 'The Army took the best of Frank and sent me back a shell of the man he was. He never talked about the war. He never really talked about anything after that.'

'That must have been hard for you,' I said, lamely wishing for something, anything, else to offer.

'He was a fine husband. A hard worker. A good provider. But he was just… broken. And when I needed him, he… well… he just wasn't really there for me.'

'How ever did you manage all those hard times on your own?' I asked, rubbing strawberry-scented lotion into the feet that had carried Doris through so much tragedy. I thought of the complete lack of misfortune in my own life and how easy we had it now.

'There wasn't a choice. There was no one else. I got up each day and put one foot in front of the other and did what needed doing. When it was all done, I'd sink into bed until it was time to get up and start all over again. It was nothing special.'

Maybe it wasn't special to Doris. Maybe that's what women did in those days. But it seemed pretty extraordinary to me. My job was all about serving the elderly with dignity. I'd do it better now, thanks to Doris.

* * * * *

On a dreary day months later, I pulled into Doris's driveway, dabbing at teary eyes and hoping my make-up had survived. I was late, thanks to Mum's early morning phone call, and concern hovered lower than the drizzly grey sky.

The walk to the front door wasn't long enough for me to muster my usual cheery disposition. We went through the motions in silence, until I once again found myself washing feet that had lived through the Depression and carried a grieving Doris on far too many lonely walks behind far too many coffins.

I needed some of Doris's courage to face Mum's diagnosis and be the daughter she needed me to be. If Doris could do it for Johnny, and all the others, I could do it for Mum – take her to the oncologist, the treatment centre, the wig shop. Because, like Doris said, there was no one else. Dad had left years ago. My sisters lived overseas.

'You okay?' Doris asked, reaching for clean socks. The hearing aides were in and I'd missed my cue to start chattering. I smiled, pleased she'd noticed.

'Just a lot on my mind today, Doris.'

'One foot in front of the other,' she whispered, patting my arm.

'Pardon.'

'That's how you face it.'

'Face what, Doris?' I hadn't told her about Mum's cancer, or my family situation. It was too soon to talk about it with anyone.

'Whatever it is that's weighing you down. Just do what you have to today. Then tomorrow, do what has to be done tomorrow.' She smiled and bent to do up her shoelaces.

I stood to let her pass as, slowly and carefully, she put one one-hundred-year-old foot in front of the other and walked to the kitchen to make breakfast.

With age comes... some final thoughts

Did you realise you're older now than you were when you started
reading this book? And that you'll be older still tomorrow?
And even older the day, the month, the year after that.
It's important to appreciate that the ageing process
happens to us all, and the way we live today helps determine
what sort of an older person we'll become.

Now, this isn't an advert for superannuation, although what you do
with your money can weigh into what sort of retirement you face.
No! I'm talking about the sort of person you are today,
and how the life you lead now impacts the life you'll have later.

If you want to look back without regret tomorrow,
be quick to apologise today.
If you don't want to be lonely tomorrow, love generously today.
If you want rich friendships, forgive freely.
If you want people around you who are prepared to spend time
with you tomorrow, spend time with them today.

I doubt many of the older people I know lived their lives always
thinking of tomorrow. It's just not practical. The now is far too
consuming, too urgent, too pressing to be thinking about tomorrow
all the time. But how honouring would it be to them if we learnt
this one thing from their lives – live today well.

And say 'I love you' more.
Because one day, far sooner than you can imagine, that person who
needs to hear it from you won't be there anymore.
And eventually, sometime, neither will you!